"You ... **neve** ...

Jason implored her. "But wasn't it the memories that brought you back here tonight? The memories of you and me on that couch, together?"

Nickie remembered. "Jason, please stop."

But he closed in, and gripped her by the shoulders. Nickie knew she couldn't deny the truth, yet she pushed him away. "Leave me my memories, Jason. Don't take even those away from me."

For a long moment, he stared at her in pained disbelief. "It really is over for you."

As Nickie watched him head toward the door, pain and loneliness filled her. She couldn't let it end like this. "Jason, no. Don't go."

He whirled and then she was in his arms. She'd almost forgotten how wonderful it felt to have him kissing her, touching her.

Both of them trembled as he picked her up, carried her to the couch. Why had she ever fought him? she wondered. *They always ended up this way. . . .*

In *Stellar Attraction*, **Eugenia Riley** explores a classic romantic fantasy and dilemma: what happens after a plain Jane wins the love of the man of her dreams? Once married, the heroine painfully discovers that the romantic notions she had of love and marriage may end up destroying any possibility of a happy ending. Eugenia and her own husband, after many years of marriage, have learned love and marriage are hard work—but the rewards are wonderful!

Books by Eugenia Riley

HARLEQUIN TEMPTATION
292—LOVE NEST
324—THE PERFECT MATE

Don't miss any of our special offers. Write to us at the following address for information on our newest releases.

Harlequin Reader Service
P.O. Box 1397, Buffalo, NY 14240
Canadian address: P.O. Box 603,
Fort Erie, Ont. L2A 5X3

Stellar Attraction

EUGENIA RILEY

Harlequin Books

TORONTO • NEW YORK • LONDON
AMSTERDAM • PARIS • SYDNEY • HAMBURG
STOCKHOLM • ATHENS • TOKYO • MILAN
MADRID • WARSAW • BUDAPEST • AUCKLAND

With love to my daughter, Noelle,
with congratulations on her graduation from high school

Published April 1992

ISBN 0-373-25491-1

STELLAR ATTRACTION

1

NICKIE STELLAR was furious.

She paced her lawyer's office, incensed and incredulous as she reread the proposed property settlement her attorney had just received from her husband's lawyer.

"Good grief!" She tossed the papers onto the desk. "Jason's contesting everything."

"Nickie, cool down," Don Amory said firmly. He was a thin, balding, mid-thirtyish man with a kindly smile.

Nickie collapsed in the chair in front of Don's desk and shakily raked a hand through her short brown hair. She had come to his office straight from her exercise class, and, with her petite, five-foot-two body encased in black tights and an oversize maroon sweater, she knew she looked more like a teenager playing hooky from school than a mature woman of twenty-six. Her round face was also youthful and pixieish, with its dark, bright eyes, upturned nose and heart-shaped mouth; yet she wore the intense, smoldering expression of an outraged woman, not that of a carefree, innocent child.

"I just can't believe he's doing this to me," she said at last, pushing up her dark-rimmed glasses. "I didn't ask Jason for *anything*. I helped him with his business. I could have asked for part of that—"

"You should have," Don reminded.

"But I didn't. I could have asked for a cash settlement, but I didn't. All I asked for was what I had before—and he's contesting even that. He wants my beach house."

"Nickie," Don interjected patiently. "The problem is, this is a joint-property state. You acquired the beach house after your marriage."

"I inherited that beach house from Aunt Grace," Nickie cut in heatedly.

Don sighed. "I know. What can I say? The man is being a jerk. I think it's pretty obvious that Jason doesn't want this divorce."

Nickie rolled her eyes. "And how!"

Don laced his long fingers together. "But there's no doubt in my mind that we'll prevail once this goes to court. Legally, Jason doesn't have a prayer. He'll pay handsomely for his arrogance."

"He's certainly arrogant."

"I just have to warn you that it looks like this case will get pretty ugly before it's over. Ultimately, though, we'll take him to the cleaners."

"But I don't want to take him to the cleaners!" Nickie argued. "I wanted to settle this quietly, out of court. I just want what's mine."

"Jason isn't going to give in without a fight," Don stated grimly.

"Okay." Nickie held her breath, trying to blink back the hot, stinging tears. "Man the torpedoes. If Jason wants to play dirty, we'll play dirty."

Don studied her closely. "Nickie, it may not be in my best interests to ask this, but are you sure you want this divorce?"

"Absolutely."

He held up a hand. "Okay. I didn't mean to upset you more. It's just that when I see this level of emotion in a client—"

"Yes?"

He shrugged. "Well, I've found that, sometimes, there's a lot more feeling left for a spouse than a client is willing to admit."

Nickie was quiet for a long moment, her thoughts turbulent. *"A lot more feeling left."* Now, that was the understatement of the century! "Would it help if I tried to reason with Jason?"

He shook his head almost violently. "You know I've advised against your having any contact with Jason—"

"But he doesn't take me seriously!" She scowled. "For that matter, he never took me seriously."

"And you think talking to him now will help?" Don asked skeptically.

She leaned forward intently. "Don, I haven't even seen Jason or spoken to him since—since that awful night at the hospital. Perhaps he still believes he can somehow manipulate himself back into my life. And maybe I'm the only person who can convince him that I mean business."

Don nodded resignedly. "You may be right. Although I usually advise a client not to have any personal contact with their spouse, it might be worth a try. But keep it to a phone call, okay?"

"Sure."

"And let me know what he says?"

"Of course."

"And, Nickie . . ."

"Yes?"

He smiled at her as they both stood. "Good luck."

She laughed ruefully as she slung the strap of her oversize black purse over her shoulder. "Thanks. I'll need all the luck I can get. I'm not sure there's any getting through to Jason—but I can try."

"I'll keep my fingers crossed."

Nickie drew a shaky breath and nodded toward the papers. "Lord knows, I can't take much more of this."

NICKIE LEFT DON'S OFFICE and drove toward her town house in west Houston. The chilly, blue November day seemed to reflect her mood. Around her, the tall buildings were shrouded in the typical haze of mist and pollution. Nickie had always found Houston to be a city of contrasts—as bleak and depressing one day as it was dazzling and bright the next.

When she arrived home, Nickie leafed through her mail and ate a sandwich. Then she sat on her overstuffed white couch, staring for a long time at the phone on the end table. This afternoon she had hoped to hear from Don that he was forging ahead with the divorce, but instead this! *Damn Jason!*

Nickie hadn't talked to him in nine months. Oh, he'd called her, sent her flowers, the whole bit. She'd refused the calls and returned the flowers. It had taken her almost six months to get up the courage to start divorce proceedings.

Now Jason was blocking her at every turn. She drew off her glasses and rubbed the bridge of her nose. She'd always felt so in awe of Jason. Theirs had been a classic mismatch—dynamic Jason Stellar and mousy little Nickie Smith. She still wasn't sure why he'd ever married her. She, however, had loved him from the instant she'd laid eyes on him. . . .

Nickie wrenched her thoughts away from dangerous territory and tried to concentrate on the issue at hand. Why was Jason so determined to fight the divorce? He'd never before seemed a vindictive person. What was driving him, then? Guilt? Stubbornness? Pride? Sexual frustration?

Nickie groaned. Certainly their love life had always been dynamite, and she missed that aspect of their relationship. Perhaps he did, too. And doubtless, he had liked having a mousy little wife waiting for him at home while he moved through his glitzy, glamorous world. But that was a role she simply wasn't willing to play anymore—not after the way he'd—

Nickie squared her jaw and forced herself to reach for the phone. Her hand trembled, then fell back. *Damn it, Nickie,* she scolded, blinking back a new wave of tears. *Get a grip and get on with this.*

Before she could lose her nerve, she grabbed the receiver and quickly punched out the numbers. Her heart pounded fiercely as the line rang.

"Stellar Attractions," came the receptionist's crisp voice.

Nickie took a bracing breath and dove in. "Jason Stellar, please."

"May I ask who's calling?"

"Nickie Stellar."

At once, the receptionist's voice grew friendlier. "Oh, yes, Mrs. Stellar. Just a minute, please. I'll put you right through."

Mrs. Stellar. Only seconds later, she heard Jason's anxious voice. "Nickie?"

Nickie was stunned by a wave of poignant feeling. Her fingers trembled on the receiver. Just hearing Jason's voice was practically enough to rip her resolve to shreds, and she was suddenly painfully aware of why she'd gone to such lengths to avoid him. It wasn't fair that any man should have such a sexy and compelling voice, she thought in despair. If just hearing him say her name did this to her, how could she ever face up to meeting him in person—if that ever became necessary?

"Nickie? Are you okay?" he prodded.

"Hello, Jason," she answered, in a tight voice.

"Well, darling, this is such a wonderful surprise," he continued smoothly. "To what do I owe the pleasure?"

Indignation bolstered Nickie's courage. "Cut the charm, Romeo," she retorted. "You know exactly why I'm calling."

"Do I?" he asked.

"I want you to stop fighting the divorce," she said heatedly.

"But, darling," he replied patiently, "I don't want the divorce. Why shouldn't I fight it?"

The word *darling* cut into her like a knife, shattering her defenses. "Jason, it's inevitable," she managed.

"Inevitable," he repeated in a silky tone. "Now that's certainly a word that applies to you and me. But it's inevitable that we end up together."

"Damn you, Jason," she said, her chest heaving. "You're not getting anywhere this time with your slick charm! You know you don't have a chance if this goes to court."

"Then let's go to court."

Exasperated, she demanded, "How can you contest my beach house in Galveston? You know Aunt Grace left it to me."

"You think I'd ever let that house go after what we shared there?"

Oh, Lord, he'd done it now, Nickie thought with a sinking heart. She was silent for a long moment, reeling from the bittersweet memories he'd awakened. At last she said, "I just want what's mine."

"Me, too." His voice was tender, almost sympathetic.

"I'm not yours anymore," she declared in a quavering voice.

His low chuckle told her he hadn't missed the quiver. "Really?"

Struggling to hang on to her determination, she blurted, "I'm seeing someone new." Stretching the truth, she added, "I want to marry him."

There was a meaningful pause, then Jason demanded, "Are you sleeping with him?"

"That's none of your business," she snapped.

"Oh, isn't it?" Now his voice was charged with outrage. "Legally, you're still my wife, Nickie. And if you *ever* want any chance of getting your divorce, you'd better tell me the truth."

Nickie hesitated, her emotions in chaos as she struggled between her justified anger at Jason and her equally justified fear of his retaliation. If she told him she was sleeping with Jim, it might convince him that things were truly over between them. It would also be a lie—a lie that could enrage Jason into fighting the divorce indefinitely.

"Okay—I'm not sleeping with him," she admitted. "I'd like to, though," she ventured recklessly. "But I draw the line at adultery, even if you don't."

"Nickie, I never betrayed you," Jason argued.

"Tell me some more lies."

"I'm not lying." His voice crackled with tension. "So you'd *like* to sleep with him, would you?"

"Yes," she reaffirmed, wanting to hurt him as much as he had hurt her.

"If it's sex you want, Nickie, I can more than satisfy you there. In fact, I can remember a time when you didn't want to sleep with anyone but me."

Nickie listened through tears. The truth was, she still didn't want to sleep with anyone but him. Only she couldn't tell him that—ever. If she did, he'd swallow her up again, and never let her go.

"Well, Nickie?" he challenged.

"Jason, stop," she said in desperation. "Let's not do this. Let's quit hurting each other. It's over. Let it go."

"No."

"For the love of heaven, isn't there any way I can reach you? Any way we can compromise? What will it take to make you back down?"

He was quiet for a long moment. "A trial reconciliation," he said at last.

"What?"

He spoke passionately. "Look, we ended things much too abruptly. We were both torn up over losing the baby, and you wouldn't even let me explain—"

"Explain?" she demanded, livid. "Explain that you came to the hospital straight from another woman's bed?"

"I didn't sleep with Tracy," he insisted. "When will you believe me?"

She laughed bitterly. "I believed the perfume I smelled on your shirt—and it sure as hell wasn't mine."

"You know I'm around other women all the time," he persisted. "There's no avoiding it in my job—"

"And there's no avoiding this divorce."

She heard his explosive sigh. Then he continued slowly, patiently, "Nickie, give the reconciliation a chance. And if it doesn't work out, I'll give you the divorce."

For the first time, Nickie found herself wavering. "And what would this . . . reconciliation . . . entail?"

"You. Back in my life—"

"And in your bed?"

"Yes," he replied bluntly.

"Go to hell, Jason," Nickie retorted, slamming down the receiver.

Blinking rapidly, she bit her lip, then hurled the phone across the room and burst into tears.

"ARE YOU ALL RIGHT, Mr. Stellar?"

At the corporate offices of Stellar Attractions, Jason's secretary burst into his office when she heard him slam down the phone and bellow a particularly vivid curse. Stephanie Burns eyed Jason with concern. He stood near the windows, staring out at the hazy skyline, his hands thrust into his pockets and his features creased in a murderous scowl. Even angry, he was a stunning man, she thought yearningly—tall, blond, blue-eyed; the very image of classic male perfection. Stephanie had only been at Stellar Attractions for a couple of months, but already, she found her boss captivating. She'd also heard he would soon be divorced—and eminently available.

"Sir?" she repeated anxiously.

Jason turned to face her, forcing a thin smile. "I'm fine, Stephanie. Sorry if I startled you."

She smiled back shyly. "Oh, no, sir. I was simply concerned. Is there anything I can get you?"

"No, thanks." He glanced at his watch. "Look, it's already past two-thirty. Why don't you call it a day and get an early start on your weekend?"

She brightened. "Are you sure, sir?"

He nodded. "We've nothing else pressing today."

"Well, in that case..." She started to leave, then turned. "Mr. Stellar, several of us at my apartment project are getting together tonight for a barbecue. What I mean is... Well, if you don't have other plans, we'd be thrilled to have you join us."

Jason raised an eyebrow in pleasant surprise. "That's very thoughtful of you, Stephanie. However... How about a rain check?"

Stephanie struggled to hide her disappointment.
"Sure, Mr. Stellar. Well, enjoy your weekend."

"You, too. And thanks."

After Stephanie left the room, Jason returned to his
desk and sat down in his leather chair with a sigh. Two
years ago, he would cheerfully have taken what the
lovely blonde had just offered—and probably, without
giving her feelings much thought. Before he'd met Nickie,
the fast lane and fast women went together for Jason
Stellar. The female sex had always found him irresistible.

Except one, who resisted him all too well.

He groaned as his thoughts returned to the telephone
conversation with his wife. It had been heavenly hearing Nickie's voice. For the first time in nine months, she
had actually spoken to him. And then he had blown it
with his arrogance and high-handed demands.

Yet it still galled him that Nickie wouldn't listen to
him, wouldn't give him—and their marriage—another
chance. He was undoubtedly a fool to continue fighting
the divorce; indeed, his attorney had already apprised
him of his idiocy on numerous occasions. Nevertheless,
the divorce proceedings offered him his last, tenuous
chance to hold on to Nickie.

He just missed her so, loved her so. What would she
say if she knew that he hadn't even gone near another
woman the entire time they'd been separated? He grimaced. That was an easy one: She wouldn't believe him.
She'd never trusted him. She'd never even believed that
she was right for him.

Yet she *was* right for him.

With growing frustration, Jason stood and walked
over to the bar. He opened a cabinet and stared at a

sealed bottle of expensive Scotch. Why had he kept the bottle all this time? To prove how strong he was?

Jason had watched alcohol destroy his parents' marriage, turning his father into a bad-tempered stranger and his mother into a long-suffering martyr. And he knew that liquor had been one significant factor in the breakup of his and Nickie's marriage. Which was why he hadn't touched a drop of booze since . . . that day. It hadn't always been easy—he'd felt tempted, on more than one occasion—and he had even gone for counseling.

He stared at the bottle and swallowed hard. Would Nickie believe he had changed—really changed—in so many ways, and that his giving up booze was just one of them? Would she believe that the separation had taught him what really mattered to him in life? *Her.*

Probably not, he reflected bitterly. And if she thought the worst of him already . . .

With a trembling hand, Jason slammed the cabinet door shut. He knew that going back to his old ways now was no answer; it would only make his problems much worse, and would make winning over Nickie impossible.

Still, the problem remained: How could he get through to her? How could he ever make her believe him or trust him, when she wouldn't even listen?

THE FOLLOWING FRIDAY morning, Don Amory called Nickie at work. "I just spoke with Jason's attorney," he began grimly. "And just as we feared, Jason's still determined to fight us tooth and nail. I'm afraid we have no choice but to battle this out in court."

"Oh, hell," Nickie muttered, trembling at the thought of seeing Jason in person again—and of fighting him—

when she had always felt so grievously outmatched by him. "Don, I'm not sure I can go through with this."

"Nickie, if you want the divorce, there's no alternative at this point."

"Isn't there something you can suggest to keep this from becoming a three-ring circus?"

"Did you talk to Jason?"

"Yes."

"Then obviously, that got us nowhere. I'm afraid there's nothing else we can do, unless—"

"Unless what?"

"Well, if you're determined to settle this without a fight—"

"Yes?"

"I don't know just what it is Jason Stellar wants from you, but I'd suggest you give it to him."

"That's out of the question," Nickie snapped.

THE REST OF THE MORNING passed in a blur for Nickie. One of her clients was being audited by the IRS the next week, but she found herself unable to concentrate on reviewing the file. Finally she gave up and just stared out her window.

The office closed at noon on Fridays, so she ducked into Jim McMurray's office to break her Saturday-night date with him. He was disappointed, and she apologized. But she was far too upset and confused right now to feel much guilt about letting him down.

Then she went home, packed her car, and headed out of the city. She had to get away. She had to think.

She'd go to her Galveston beach house.

2

IT WAS ALMOST four o'clock by the time Nickie turned off the interstate and headed for the west end of Galveston Island. Aunt Grace's beach house was in a section of homes not far from San Luis Pass at the westernmost tip of the island. The houses on this section of West Bay were set high on stilts, since this part of the island was at sea level. She turned onto the sandy driveway and parked under the cottage. As she emerged from her car, the brisk Gulf breeze wafted over her, smelling of salt and fish and refuse. Beyond her, across the sandy beach, the gray waters of the Gulf were turbulent and frothed with whitecaps.

Nickie retrieved her overnight case and groceries. Juggling her load, she cautiously mounted the weathered outdoor steps of the cottage. Nickie had always loved her Aunt Grace's house, with its cheerful yellow facade and teal-blue front door and shutters.

Inside, she studied the familiar, cozy room with its wood floor and large woven rug, the long rattan couch with cheery chintz cushions and the matching chairs, the freestanding metal fireplace. She remembered herself and Jason making love on that couch as the fire crackled....

Nickie shook herself from her traitorous memories and forced herself into action. She put the groceries away in the galley kitchen and unpacked her things in one of the two bedrooms. She swept the floors and wiped down the furniture with a dustrag, then opened the windows to catch the Gulf breeze.

Afterward, she built a fire and settled on the couch with a snifter of brandy. The thick paperback novel she'd brought along lay untouched beside her glasses on the coffee table, as she sat listening to the roar of the surf and staring numbly at the snapping flames.

What was she going to do about Jason? He'd said he wouldn't give up this beach house because of what they'd shared here, and his words still squeezed her heart like a vise.

Why was he fighting the divorce so hard? Surely by now, he had to know they were doomed.

She didn't want to remember. But how much longer could she hold those memories at bay? In fact, why else had she come here—to the place where the very walls seemed to throb with their shared, turbulent passion? Was she still subconsciously holding on to their marriage? To that brief, tumultuous year that had been so glorious—and so devastating?

There were times when she cursed the day she'd met Jason Stellar. And yet, in her heart, she knew she wouldn't have missed knowing him for the world....

SHE WAS TWENTY-FOUR when she first met Jason Stellar, that fall two years ago. After putting in two killing years at a Big Eight accounting firm, she'd finally gotten her CPA and landed a position with the midsize firm, Hawkins and Cunningham. Stellar Attractions, the small but up-and-coming women's clothing-store chain, was her first major account.

She would never forget the day she went to Jason's corporate headquarters to convince him that Hawkins and Cunningham should handle his expanding accounting needs. Jason's Houston offices were small but posh, located in a high rise in the heart of the Magic Circle. His beautiful blond secretary had come out to greet Nickie at the reception desk and showed her into his inner office. Jason at once sprang up from behind his desk, looking absolutely dazzling.

"You must be Miss Smith," he said.

"And you must be Mr. Stellar," she said.

From the moment she shook his large, strong hand, Nickie was mesmerized. Jason Stellar was undoubtedly the most handsome, charming hunk of a man she'd ever seen in her life. He was tall—easily six-two—blue-eyed, blond and trimly muscular; she felt slightly intimidated, having to stare up at him. Still, his manner was friendly and reassuring, his eyes sparkled with ready humor, and his smile was irresistible. She mused that it was downright unfair that any man should have teeth so perfect and white, or hair so thick and shiny, or eyelashes so long and sexy.

The man was a born entrepreneur, and listening to him, Nickie could easily discern how he'd taken a small women's clothing store called Brown Brothers and was turning it into a successful chain—Stellar Attractions. Nickie hung on his every word, as he detailed his plans. The Houston economy was still struggling to rebound from the oil-industry downturn, and the off-price chains were threatening the profits of his stores, just as they threatened so many other traditional retailers. But "glitz at the right price" was selling, and Stellar Attractions offered glamour in every price range to a female population bone-weary of lean times.

Jason told her how he'd built up his three Houston stores, how the finances had become too complex for the bookkeeping service he currently used, and how he'd decided he needed a CPA on call each week. He asked her about her background and qualifications, and she told him how she had graduated from Texas A&M University at the top of her class, how she'd gotten her MBA from the University of Texas, and of her two years of work experience before joining Hawkins and Cunningham.

"I'm impressed," Jason said, leaning back in his leather chair and lacing his hands behind his head. "You know, I've been debating between farming out more of my accounting needs, or hiring a full-time controller. How would Hawkins and Cunningham feel if I tried to woo you away?"

His words left Nickie blushing at the sensual undercurrent she detected in his tone. Then she chided herself for her foolishness. What would this magnificent man want with plain, boring little Nickie Smith? Wouldn't he laugh if he knew that, at twenty-four, she was still a virgin? She thought of the glamorous blonde in the outer office and mentally kicked herself again. Jason Stellar doubtless had a little black book just bursting with the names of females every bit as dazzling—and no doubt as available—as his secretary.

"Oh, I'm sure we can serve your needs without going to such extremes," Nickie said at last, and he chuckled.

By the time their meeting had concluded, it was late afternoon, and Jason surprised her by asking her out to dinner. When she protested, he said, "Please, let's seal our new partnership. And on the way, I can show you my Galleria store."

Nickie had been inside the Galleria Stellar Attractions store many times before, but she wasn't about to say so to Jason. Indeed, she felt as if she were seeing the Galleria itself for the first time as she strode down the gleaming walkway beside the gorgeous Jason Stellar. Being so short, she practically had to jog to keep up with his long-legged stride, and the long sprint down the cat-walk toward his store heightened her feeling of breath-less anticipation. The other shoppers, even the skaters gliding down the center rink, seemed to float past her in a haze. Nickie had eyes only for Jason Stellar, and she sorely wished she'd worn something more spectacular than her drab brown suit.

Inside his store, Nickie watched Jason in action. The salesgirls' faces were wreathed in smiles as they called out, "Hi, Mr. Stellar!" Jason grinned back and greeted each girl by name, and that's when Nickie noticed that he had dimples—the cutest dimples she'd ever seen on a man.

Jason showed her his innovative merchandising tech-niques—the chrome mannequins and tasteful track lighting, the ingenious displays of glamorous women's clothing and accessories in every price range. Nickie practically drooled over the holiday stock just in from New York. Jason introduced her to his manager and as-sistant managers, acquainting her with their opera-tions. She felt about eight feet tall. She asked him questions, which he answered in detail, delighted by her interest.

Afterward, Jason surprised her by taking her to dine at elegant Maxim's downtown. He was charming, al-most flirtatious, and Nickie reflected that if she hadn't known better, she would suspect that Jason Stellar was trying to seduce her. Seduce her, indeed! What would he want with skinny little Nickie Smith, with her plain, round face, her short, lusterless hair and her dark-rimmed glasses? He'd probably just had no plans for the evening and was desperate for company.

But when he reached out during the meal and placed his hand over hers, she began to reconsider. "Do you have a husband, Nickie?" he asked.

"No," she replied tremulously.

"A boyfriend?"

"No."

"No one?"

"I—er— It's sort of been a busy life for me," she said at last, and felt ridiculous when he threw back his head and laughed. "I mean, first I had to get my degree, then my MBA—"

"Ah, yes. You're one of those brainy types who graduated magna cum laude—"

"Summa," she amended, and he laughed again. Clearing her throat, she continued, "Then I had to land my first job, and work toward my CPA—"

"A busy life," he concurred, grinning at her. "But what do you do when you want to have fun?"

She shrugged. "Well, I have some friends I do things with—"

He squeezed her hand. "Would you like another one?"

"Yes, that would be nice," she said primly, barely able to speak over the pounding of her heart.

He chuckled, shaking his head. "Nickie, you're priceless."

As they drank coffee and ate their luscious desserts, Nickie found herself wondering if Jason would suggest they stop off for a nightcap or go to his place later—and chided herself that the champagne must be going to her head. To her disappointment, he was courtesy personified as he drove her back to his office building and parked his Mercedes convertible next to her small subcompact. "Nickie, it's been great," he said as he strode around to open her door. "We must do this again soon."

"Sure, Jason. Thanks for everything," she said with a brave smile. To herself, she added, *Sure, I've heard that line before.* They stared at each other for an awkward moment. Nickie reached out to shake his hand. "Good night. I look forward to working with you." Then, with a wan smile, she swept past him toward her car.

Nickie's spirits sagged as she drove home. She felt certain that, for Jason Stellar, having dinner with her had been just a wise business move, a chance to get better acquainted with a new associate.

During the next week, the two of them were together a lot as she helped him prepare his annual budget. They became much better acquainted, both personally and professionally, and he insisted that she have lunch with him twice. He made no move to kiss her—but the way he stared at her so often, the way he clutched her arm as they swept through a doorway, the way he occasionally caught her hand and squeezed it, all seemed to hint that he wanted more than just a business relationship, or even a casual friendship, with her. When he asked her to have dinner with him on Friday night, she *knew* Jason Stellar was attracted to her.

This time he took her to Vargo's in west Houston; they sipped white wine and ate shrimp tempura. Jason told her of how he was thinking of expanding his business to Dallas and San Antonio. "Now that you're familiar with my operations, what do you think?"

She was thrilled that her opinion mattered so much to him. "I'd say you've built up a solid base here in Houston, in a very tough market. There's no reason for you not to expand, although arranging for the additional venture capital might be a problem. You don't want to risk going into a new market undercapitalized."

He nodded. "I know. But I've a good relationship with my banker, and I don't think gaining the additional financing will be a problem. Of course, scouting locations for the stores and assessing the viability of potential new markets could be quite a challenge."

"It sounds like fun to me," Nickie pointed out. "Being in on the ground floor, the planning stages, of an exciting new venture."

"I'll bet it would be fun for you, being so knowledgeable and bright." He touched her hand. "Nickie, would you come with me? Help me do some of the groundwork in San Antonio and Dallas?"

She was at once both elated and taken aback. "Well... I..."

"I really value your opinion," he said sincerely. "And I'd enjoy having you with me."

Nickie practically choked on her breadstick. "Of course, then, Jason. I'd be thrilled to help you."

He grinned. "I can tell that this venture is going to be both interesting and lots of fun." Watching her blush and stare at him, wide-eyed, he shook his head. "Nickie, you're delightful."

As they discussed their plans over coffee, Nickie decided that Jason Stellar was the man she wanted to give her virginity to. Because he was suave, debonair, gorgeous—everything she wasn't. And because he was the only man she'd ever met who'd called her "delightful."

Of course, she had no illusions about what the night would mean to him. They'd been thrown together because of business, and certainly they'd become friends. But beyond that, the sex would be little more than an enjoyable side benefit to him.

Still, he was so charming and attractive, and she wanted him terribly. She was twenty-four years old, and she was tired of carrying her virginity around like some sort of portable shrine. During the past two years, she'd been far too busy trying to get ahead to think much about romance. Prior to that, while she'd been in college, she'd been put off by the shallowness and immaturity of most of the men she met—and most of them had been put off by her brains. But not Jason Stellar. He found her "delightful."

Leaving the restaurant, Jason caressed the curve of her cheek with his knuckles and said softly, "Care to come to my place for a nightcap?"

They both knew exactly what the invitation meant. "Yes," Nickie replied without hesitation.

At his condominium they sat by the fire, sipping brandy and listening to Elton John. Nickie drank a little too much, and she had a feeling Jason was getting a little high, too. After a while, he took her snifter and his and placed them on the coffee table. Then he stared at her, a devastating smile tugging at his beautiful mouth. She would absolutely *die* if he didn't kiss her soon.

"You know, there comes a moment in every movie when a man takes off the lady's glasses," he said. He paused to demonstrate, then murmured, "Hey, you really shouldn't hide behind these. You're lovely."

Nickie was embarrassed. "I'm not," she said, turning away.

His hand caught her chin, turning her toward him. "But of course you are—with that cute little upturned nose and those big brown eyes. Not to mention that perky little mouth . . ."

"Perky?" she repeated indignantly.

Then Jason was kissing that "perky" mouth, and Nickie was soaring. She felt as if she'd waited an eternity to taste the hot pleasure of his lips on hers. He drew her across the couch into his lap. It was heavenly, having him hold her that way, as if she were cherished. Fire sizzled along her veins as his mouth worked its wonder and his tongue seduced hers. She moaned and kissed him back recklessly, thrusting her tongue inside his mouth, feeling delighted by his hoarse moan.

"You're so slim," he said, clutching her tightly against him.

She laughed breathlessly, feeling dizzy as she caught a lungful of his intoxicating scent. "I'm skinny as a rail."

"Bite your tongue, woman," he scolded, nibbling at her neck. "You're perfect." He unbuttoned the top button on her dress. "How tall are you?"

"Five-two."

"You seem smaller."

"That's because I'm so thin—"

"Perfect," he growled, and she gasped in response as his hand caressed her breast. Then that same, wonderful hand moved to caress her leg, and Nickie could hardly breathe. Even though his fingers were resting just above her knee, hot tentacles of desire pierced deep into the very core of her, making her achy and light-headed.

"I love your little body," he murmured. "I'm used to tall, leggy models—"

She stiffened, and he pulled back to smile at her. "Strictly in a business way, of course."

Nickie rolled her eyes. "Oh, of course."

He seemed to sense her doubt, for he planted tender kisses on her face. "Nickie, darling, I want you so much. Let's make this a night we'll both remember always."

And Nickie was lost.

In the darkened bedroom, Jason tore feverishly at her clothes, popping a button on her dress. "I'm sorry," he murmured as his hand reached for her hem. Then, pulling off her dress and slip, he feasted his eyes on her and whistled. "No, I'm not. I'll buy you a new dress— Hell, I'll buy you ten."

"Just hush and kiss me," she gasped, shocking herself with her own boldness as she pressed her parted lips on his and reached for the buttons of his shirt. As his mouth again drank hungrily of hers, she thrust open the shirt and spread her fingers over his taut muscles and crisp hair. "You're beautiful," she said reverently, leaning over to kiss the hollow of his chest.

"So are you," he murmured, and with a satisfied growl, took her nipple into his mouth. She uttered a soft cry, instinctively arching at the unbearable rapture she felt. But Jason only chuckled and thrust his hands inside her panties to pull her to him, digging his fingers into her buttocks. Nickie reeled at his provocative touch, feeling gooseflesh break out all over her body. His bold hands lifted her against his hardness, even as his wonderful mouth deepened the wet, hot pressure at her breast. Nickie was going insane, breathing in short, painful gasps and thrusting her fingers through the silken texture of his hair. She had never known such pleasure could exist, that she could be inflamed by a need so intense, it actually hurt deep in the pit of her stomach. She trembled against him and murmured, "Oh, yes," and was rewarded when his hands impatiently tugged off her remaining clothes. She felt completely vulnerable to him then, and loved the feeling—loved knowing that she would give over a part of herself to him.

She would never forget the electrifying moment when they fell across the bed together, both naked and breathing hard. Jason felt so muscular, so warm, so strong, so overwhelmingly male. His rough chest abraded her soft, aroused breasts in a way that was electrifyingly sensual.

She kissed him hungrily, deeply; she just couldn't get enough of him. He kissed her back so fiercely that their teeth ground together, yet neither cared.

Soon, she wanted him inside her so desperately, she was close to sobbing from sheer frustration. She couldn't say the words, so she grabbed his hand and pressed it low against her belly. He understood at once and smiled down at her as he massaged that aching part of her. When his fingers parted her thighs, she tossed her head and struggled to breathe. Then he stroked her and she writhed against his hand. He took her hand then, guiding it to his arousal, and her eyes widened in shocked pleasure as she clutched the large, hard shaft. Trying to imagine that vast hardness inside her, she gasped with an emotion that was half fear, half anticipation. Should she tell him? she wondered. No. If he knew she was a virgin, he might stop. Maybe she could get through this without his knowing.

No such luck. Soon, he was pressing against her with the straining tip of his penis, and getting nowhere. "Nickie?" he demanded raggedly. "Good Lord! Don't tell me I'm your first?"

"Yes," she whispered miserably, clinging to him. "But please don't stop."

He chuckled. "You think I would stop?"

"I want you. Please," she said.

He pulled back and stared down at her a moment. The look in his eyes was so tender, she practically drowned in its sweetness. "Oh, darling. But why me?"

Tears sprang to her eyes. "Because you said I was delightful."

"Oh, Nickie. You are. But—you're not on the Pill, are you?"

She shook her head. "Still, I don't think I'll get pregnant tonight— I mean, it's not the right time of the month—"

"That sounds too chancy to me. Hold on a minute, darling."

He left her momentarily. When he returned and pressed against her again, he was slick this time and managed an initial, painful entry. "Oh, love," he whispered, kissing the tears on her eyelashes, "I know it hurts. You're so tiny and tight—"

"Please love me, Jason," she gasped.

"You couldn't stop me now if you wanted to."

But nothing could stop the pain of that initial consummation. He was patient and loving, but she was small and untried. Finally, he placed his hands beneath her and surged hard to see an end to it. A tearing pain shot through her, and she buried her face against his shoulder, trembling and clinging to him. The pressure of him inside her was unbearably intense, yet equally wondrous. Despite the discomfort, she gloried in the intimacy, the total sharing, and she arched instinctively against him, struggling to take him deeper.

"Oh, darling—you're so sweet," he said raggedly.

Jason tried to be gentle, but soon Nickie's eagerness, her tear-filled kiss, shattered his control. He uttered a feral groan and ended it with several quick, deep strokes, and she shuddered against him. She felt so close to him then, and yet she also felt as if some elemental breakthrough had just eluded her. Still, when he withdrew from her, she felt bereft....

Afterward, he prepared a bath for her, to let the soreness ease from her body, and then held her close all night. But he didn't make love to her again.

THE NEXT MORNING, they were like two strangers staring at each other over the breakfast table. At last Jason reached out and took her hand. "You okay?"

She nodded, afraid that if she spoke, she would cry. She was sure she must have disappointed him last night. It had all been so quick and awkward, and she had to admit that she felt somewhat disappointed, herself. Obviously, she just wasn't a passionate woman.

"Why me, Nickie?" Jason asked.

She stared at him, feeling color rise in her face. "I thought I explained that last night."

He laughed ruefully. "You hang on to your virginity for twenty-four years, and then, just like that, you give it to me?"

She glanced up at him resentfully. "Look, Jason, we've become good friends over the past weeks. But if you're afraid I might try to obligate you in some way, forget it. You don't owe me anything."

He scowled at that. "So I'm just some convenient guy to initiate you into sex?"

"I think we both went into last night with our eyes open."

He was still frowning, about to comment, when the phone rang. He grabbed the receiver impatiently. "Hello?" he barked. "Yes, Melissa. Look, this isn't a good time for me to talk. I don't know about tonight. Can I call you back?"

He hung up the phone and they stared at each other tensely. "So, where do we go from here, Nickie?" he asked.

She shrugged. "Why don't you call Melissa back and confirm your date for tonight?"

"That happens to be business, and I may just cancel it," he answered heatedly.

"Don't let me change your life."

"But you have. You changed it when you came here last night."

"What is this?" she asked, gesturing in nervous frustration. "Some latent sense of honor? I thought it was missing in twentieth-century men."

"Well, think again. I know very few men who wouldn't feel very taken aback to have a twenty-four-year-old virgin come to their bed, then get up the next morning and say it meant nothing—"

"Jason, please," she said, twisting her fingers together miserably. "It meant something. It meant a lot."

"Did it?"

He was already half out of his chair when she stood and raised her hand. "Look, I'm really glad you were the one. But you've got your life, I've got mine, and I think it's time for me to go."

"Go?" he asked angrily. "So what are you going to do, Nickie, now that I've divested you of the inconvenience of your virginity? Go find some other guy to—"

The word he used was coarse and graphic. Outraged, she raised her hand to slap him, and the next thing she knew, he had grabbed it and hauled her into his arms. "Don't go, Nickie," he said tenderly. "Spend the weekend with me."

Tears sprang to Nickie's eyes, and she shuddered with joy. He'd just said the very words she most longed to hear. "But, why?"

He raised her chin and looked down into her brimming eyes. "Because I find you delightful," he said. "And, damn it, because I can't stand the idea of you being with anyone else." And his mouth closed over hers in a hard, possessive kiss.

She spent the rest of the weekend with him. They held hands at the top of the Transco Tower and ate dinner at elegant Tony's, where Jason kissed her at their intimate corner table, between bites of caviar and sips of champagne. Back at his condominium, he held her in his arms, but he didn't make love to her. She felt hurt and confused.

But the next morning, she awakened to find Jason pulling off the T-shirt that she'd slept in. With the heavy line of whiskers along his jaw and the determined gleam in his eye, he looked deliciously sexy, and hot desire raced along her every nerve.

"I know you're probably still sore," he whispered, kissing her. "But I don't think I can live another minute without making love to you again."

"Oh, Jason," she cried, throwing her arms around his neck. "I thought you were disappointed—"

"Disappointed? Do you have any idea what hell it's been for me to keep my hands off you?" He drew her hand to his erection. "Does this feel like disappointment to you?"

She grinned wickedly. "It feels like just what I want."

His eyes glittered with a smoldering light then, but still he took his time, working his lips down her body. The abrasion of his bearded face felt marvelous against her tender breasts, her bare stomach.

"I want you very aroused," he said thickly as he tugged off her panties. "That should help."

She laughed. "I get *very* aroused just looking at you."

Yet Nickie discovered new definitions for the word as Jason pressed his face between her thighs. The sensual contrast between his rough, bearded face and delicate lips and tongue drove her to the brink of madness, to new, unbelievable heights of arousal and frustration.

Soon he was clamping both arms low on her belly just to hold her still. Her voice grew hoarse with pleading and she tugged at his hair, begging him to kiss her, to bring them together. At last he positioned himself above her, thrusting his tongue into her mouth as she eagerly wrapped her legs about his waist and stroked him boldly.

This time Jason was unhurried as he pressed fully into her tight, warm sheath. He stared down into her flushed face, watching her pupils dilate as he increased her excitement with slow, deep thrusts. His deliberateness drove her mad, and soon she became a wild woman, clawing at him, begging for release. He only laughed and rolled over, pulling her on top of him. Nickie gasped as the new position locked their bodies even more intimately.

"Make love to me, tigress," he whispered.

Staring down into his passion-glazed eyes, Nickie clutched his shoulders and began to move against him, tentatively at first, then with growing fervor and abandon. Her eagerness and uninhibited movements unleashed the wildness in him. Nickie's fingernails dug into his shoulders as she felt herself slipping away into a new realm of endless, searing pleasure. Just as his release came, she clenched about him in a climax so intense, it left her weeping in his arms.

He didn't have to ask whether her tears were of pain or pleasure. He knew.

3

OVER THE NEXT FEW WEEKS they'd spent all their free time together. Jason was charming, thoughtful, passionate, and Nickie was falling desperately in love with him. She feared she was setting herself up for a terrible fall, but she couldn't stop herself.

As far as his business was concerned, Jason soon came to depend on her. She centralized his inventory and ordering procedures, establishing a computer base for all three stores. She accompanied him on trips to Dallas and San Antonio to scout locations for his new stores. Nickie found the groundwork exciting and Jason took her advice seriously.

Still, she puzzled over *why* Jason was interested in her.

Then came the day when he invited her to meet him at his southwest Houston store. A salesgirl led her to a back room where Jason stood with two women—a middle-aged matron in a suit, and a tall, beautiful model who wore little more than high-heeled sandals and a slip. The room was thick with the woman's perfume—a sickeningly sweet floral mix. On a nearby rack were two glittery cocktail gowns.

"Ah, Nickie!" Jason strode over and took her arm. "You're just in time to give us some advice. What do you think Tracy should wear for our winter show? The green silk—" he paused to hold the shimmering dress in front of the model "—or the red taffeta?"

Nickie glanced at Tracy—she was willowy and slim, dark and exotically beautiful. She was studying Nickie with assessing, heavily made-up eyes. Then the model's gaze shifted to Jason, and she stared at him as if he were a luscious confection she was about to devour.

"I'd say green suits her," Nickie murmured.

"Just what Monica and I were thinking," Jason agreed with a broad grin. He wrapped his arm about Nickie's waist. "Isn't she a marvel?" he asked the other two women.

They responded with desultory compliments, and soon afterward, Jason and Nickie left. As they strode back through the suburban mall, Nickie was preoccupied. Finally, Jason stopped her. "Darling, what's wrong?"

"Are you always around half-naked models?" she asked.

He chuckled. "I'm charmed that you feel jealous." As she glowered at him, he added, "You know we have frequent fashion shows at Stellar Attractions. And when I'm trying to match a model with an outfit, it's ridiculous to have her leave the room every time she changes."

"I suppose you're right." She bit her lip. "I guess I didn't realize that you took such a personal interest in—well, the creative end of your business."

"How do you think I made Stellar Attractions what it is today?" He squeezed her hand as they continued walking. "And don't worry. Like I told you, it's only business."

"I think it was more than business to Tracy."

He raised an eyebrow at that. "Oh?"

"I think she's attracted to you."

He laughed. "Really? I hadn't even noticed."

Nickie harrumphed. "You're bound to have noticed her perfume. It almost knocked me dead. What was it, anyway?"

"Some custom mix she likes. Awful, wasn't it?"

They strolled along for a moment, then Nickie lowered her voice and asked intently, "Have you slept with her?"

He appeared stunned. "Don't be ridiculous."

"Have you?"

"No," he said vehemently.

"But you've slept with other models?"

He stared at the window of a shop they were passing, raking a hand through his hair and looking highly uncomfortable.

"Jason?" She tugged on his sleeve and stopped him.

"Okay, so I have," he admitted at last. As she glanced away to cover her pain, he drew her into his arms and added in a passionate whisper, "Darling, I haven't slept with anyone else since skinny little Nickie Smith seduced me."

"Seduced you?" she repeated in an indignant hiss, her gaze flashing upward to meet his. "I seduced you?"

He grinned. "Yes, ma'am."

"And now I'm skinny?"

"Your choice of word," he said with a devilish wink. "And I think I'm beginning to get used to it."

"And to 'tall, leggy models,'" she quoted.

He leaned intimately toward her and whispered, "Your legs wrap around me perfectly. And there's a part of you that's even more perfect—"

"Jason, stop it," she said, feeling embarrassed as a couple of passing shoppers stared pointedly at them.

While Jason only chuckled and led her on toward the exit, Nickie felt perturbed. Was what they had purely physical? Was it because he'd been her first, that he was determined that she not sleep with anyone else?

Nickie decided it would be best to pull back from Jason. She found herself avoiding him, making excuses, breaking dates. Whenever her resolve weakened, she remembered her parents' troubled marriage. Her mom had been plain, like herself, yet she'd married a handsome, dynamic, real-estate developer. The marriage had always been haunted by jealousy and suspicion. Then, when Nickie was only fourteen, her gorgeous dad had walked out on his wife and three children, running off with a woman half his age. Four years after the breakup, her mom had remarried—to a fine but ordinary man. And she'd been happy ever since.

That's where Nickie knew she belonged, too—with a safe, ordinary man. Not with a "stellar attraction" like Jason Stellar.

However, getting Jason out of her life—and, especially, out of her thoughts—proved far more difficult than Nickie had anticipated. The solution was to find someone new to date, someone to take her mind off Jason. Finding a prospect wasn't easy, until one day, when a new client walked into her office. He was a big, awkward Texan named Hank Stetson, and he called her "little lady" and hung on every word she said. Nickie couldn't help but be impressed when he told her his rags-to-riches tale—how his oil-tool business had "busted out" four years ago, and how he'd regained financial stability by doing contract machine work for the aerospace industry. Even though Stetson Machining wasn't a large account, Nickie encouraged Hank's business and even asked him out to lunch.

They were laughing over their coffee and desserts, when Jason strode in. He approached their table, smiling, but Nickie could tell by the tautness of his expression that he was furious. When he stood beside her, her heart stopped for an agonizing split second, then beat harder than a kettledrum.

"Hello, Nickie," Jason said blandly. "Your office told me you'd be here."

"What are you doing here?" she asked in bewilderment.

"Aren't you going to introduce me to your friend?" he went on smoothly.

In one of the most awkward moments of her life, Nickie introduced Jason Stellar to Hank Stetson. To Jason, she added pointedly that Hank was a new client.

"Ah, yes. Nickie's such a wonderful little accountant," Jason remarked to Hank. "In fact, that's why I had to intrude on your little tête-à-tête. I'm afraid there's been an emergency at my corporate offices. Our computer ate up the entire Friday payroll. So, you don't mind if I abscond with Nickie, do you, Hank?"

"Now, wait just a minute, Jason," Nickie interjected, not believing his trumped-up tale for an instant.

"Hey, ma'am, no problem," Hank said graciously. "We're just about finished up here, anyway, aren't we? I mean, if there's a genuine emergency for Mr. Stellar, here—"

"Oh, there is," Jason replied.

Nickie was seething by the time she left the restaurant with Jason. "Just what was that nonsense about?" she demanded as he ushered her into his Mercedes. "You know damn well that you use an outside payroll service."

He walked around to the driver's side, got in and slammed the door. "I don't share what's mine."

Nickie almost choked in her indignation. "Yours? How dare you presume I'm some—some possession of yours!"

"Why have you been avoiding me, Nickie?"

"I—I've been busy," she stammered.

His crude rejoinder burned her ears, and the tires squealed as his car shot away from the curb.

"So where's the fire, Jason?" she asked.

"Guess."

Her jaw dropped. "Of all the arrogant, presumptuous—"

"Are you sleeping with him?" he asked angrily.

"Him?"

"Hank Houston."

"Hank Stetson. And he's just a client."

"So was I. Are you sleeping with him?"

"That's none of your damned—"

The tires squealed again, and Jason narrowly missed hitting another car as he pulled them up to a curb. He turned to her with chest heaving and blue eyes blazing. "Damn it, Nickie, I've never before shaken a woman. Maybe I'm a complete fool, but I actually thought we meant something to each other. So if you don't level with me right this instant—"

"No," she cried.

"No, what?"

"No, I'm not sleeping with him."

The rest of the trip passed in silence until they were inside his condominium. The tension stretched between them. Nickie could barely meet Jason's gaze. At last he asked, "If you're not having an affair with him, then why do you look so guilty?"

Nickie almost fell apart then. She loved Jason so much, but she was so afraid. He could never feel as strongly about her as she did about him. He was simply caught up in the emotion of their affair.

"Nickie?" he prodded.

"Because I was thinking about it," she admitted in a small voice.

He turned white with anger, yet his eyes gleamed with hurt. "Why?"

Tears began to spill from her eyes. "To get you out of my mind."

He drew a step closer, and when he spoke, his voice was much gentler. "Why?"

She clenched then unclenched her fists. "Because I have to break away. Because I love you. Because I can't have you."

"Idiot," he murmured, and caught her roughly in his arms.

All she could feel was his arms as they trembled about her, his lips as they ravished hers, his need as he pulled her to the couch and pressed her down.

They made love with reckless, desperate passion. "Are you okay?" he asked afterward.

"Yes," she whispered.

He grinned. "Sometimes I forget that you're still kind of new at this."

Then he carried her to the bedroom, where they made love a second and a third time. When she awakened later, he was gone; she found him in the living room on the phone. "Seven o'clock. Hey, that's great," he was saying as he stood. "Yes, we'll be there."

Nickie eyed him sleepily. "We'll be where?"

"At the airport tonight. We're flying to Vegas and getting married."

As Nickie gasped, Jason lost his usual confidence. "That is," he said tentatively, "if you'll have me, Nickie."

If she'd have him! Nickie whooped in joy. She flew across the room into his arms, almost knocking him off his feet. She kissed him with feverish happiness.

Then, tentatively, she said, "Jason, you don't have to do this because you were my first—"

"Nickie, I'm doing this because I love you."

Then he grabbed her and swung her around, and they both laughed until they cried.

AT FIRST, MARRIAGE to Jason had been great, although Nickie often worried that perhaps they'd rushed into things too soon. Still, during those early months, they spent every free moment together, and stole more. Nickie quit her job at Hawkins and Cunningham and devoted herself full-time to helping Jason with his business. Of course, they had their occasional spats—especially being together almost twenty-four hours a day—but the making up afterward was glorious. They couldn't get enough of each other.

Then, when Jason decided to open the stores in Dallas and San Antonio simultaneously, the preparation was practically killing them both. On top of that, he was expanding two of his Houston stores. Jason was determined to double his business before they started a family, and, with typical entrepreneurial zeal, he wanted everything *now*.

That was when the problems began: Nickie got tired of flying all over the state with him, and someone was needed to run operations at home. Nickie also discovered that, while she loved being in on the planning stages of a new shop and was fascinated by the inner workings of Jason's business, she was strictly a behind-the-scenes person and hated the limelight. Thus, as the openings of the new stores drew near—when Jason started lining up trunk shows, arranging publicity, meeting with factory representatives and hiring staff—Nickie found herself shying away.

Jason was of course disappointed that she didn't travel with him as much, but understood that his Houston operations would suffer without her at the helm. Still, he was gone more and more, and he began to drink heavily. When Nickie complained, he accused her of nagging and said, "I'm doing this for us. We're both working toward our future, Nickie."

When he was home, he still couldn't get enough of her, but resentment and mistrust continued to build between them. Nickie knew that Jason spent most of his time with beautiful women—women buyers, women manufacturer's representatives, women store managers, women models. She was jealous, and fearful of her ability to hold on to Jason. Sometimes she smelled perfume on his clothing. One time she confronted him about it, and he muttered something offhanded about a meeting with a representative from Estée Lauder.

When Nickie's aunt died and left her the beach house, she began to spend time alone there. Jason came with her once or twice, but mostly she went by herself.

Then one night, he came home to their condo in Houston with lipstick on his collar, and something in Nickie broke. She walked out without saying a single word to him, and drove like a demon, straight to the beach house.

She didn't realize he'd followed her until he was banging at her door. When she let him in, he was livid. "Do you know you drove down here like a maniac? You could have been killed, Nickie!"

"Would you have cared?"

He looked incredulous. "Would I have cared? Nickie, what's wrong with you?"

She seethed with indignation. "The damned lipstick on your collar, that's what's wrong with me!"

He yanked at his shirt collar, popping a button, then stared at the smudge. "That?"

"*That* is called grounds for divorce, mister."

"Nickie, you don't understand. Today I opened a new account with Henry Lamont. He's a new clothing manufacturer back east. I guess their representative got a bit . . . exuberant."

"Quit lying to me, Jason."

"I'm not lying."

"You come home, reeking of perfume—"

"I'm around perfume—and women—all day. And, again, that kiss was perfectly innocent. Look, Sally Gideon, the factory rep, is still in Houston. If you like, we'll call her at her hotel."

"Okay, okay," Nickie conceded. "Maybe that particular kiss was innocent. But how many haven't been?"

"Only ours, darling," he said, taking her in his arms and, then, as always, Nickie was a goner.

"So I really made you that jealous," he murmured, kissing her nose. "You know my life is an open book to you, Nickie. You're welcome to come along any time."

"I can't be with you every minute," she argued petulantly.

"I know that. But why can't you trust me?"

She bit her lip. She couldn't force herself to say, *Because I never could figure out why you would want someone like me.* "I just wish you were around more," she said instead.

"I'm around now," he replied, flashing her his sexy, dazzling smile. "And I think it's about time for me to prove to my very jealous wife that I've brought it all home to her."

He did. He loved her until she could barely move, barely breathe. And he got her pregnant that night.

JASON WAS BESIDE HIMSELF when the doctor confirmed Nickie's pregnancy. It was Christmastime, and a happier Christmas two people have never known. For a week, it was like old times—Nickie and Jason together almost every minute, planning the nursery, buying the layette.

Then Jason started redoubling his efforts to expand his business. He wanted everything to be perfect before the baby arrived. The new stores were not taking off as well as he had anticipated, and his personal supervision was required more and more. He was gone more than ever, and several times he left his car at the airport and came home late at night in a taxi, dead drunk. Nickie was alarmed, but prayed that Jason would get a grip on himself once the new stores got off the ground.

Late one night, she awakened to feel his mouth on hers. He tasted heavily of Scotch. "No, Jason," she said, pushing him away. "You're drunk."

"I want you, Nickie," he said, kissing her again.

They grappled briefly, his strength frightening her. "No, Jason!" she pleaded. "Not like this."

"Okay," he said, rolling away.

The next morning, she confronted him. "I don't want to have sex with you again until after the baby's born. You were drunk last night and you could have hurt me— or the baby."

He looked so genuinely wounded, she almost retracted her words. "Did I hurt you?" he asked in a strangled tone.

"No. But you could have."

For the first time, she spotted angry tears in Jason Stellar's eyes. "Get something straight, Nickie. I'd never, *ever* hurt you—or our child."

And he walked out the door, slamming it behind him.

FROM THAT POINT ONWARD, they were estranged. Jason didn't touch her, and Nickie was too proud to go to him. He still drank too much, he was still gone too much of the time.

The charged atmosphere at home soon convinced her that for the sake of the baby, she should move out. She'd also experienced some spotting and cramping early in her pregnancy, and her doctor, too, urged her to avoid all possible emotional stress. Afraid of Jason's response, she didn't tell him the day she moved out into a town house she had leased; he was away from Houston, anyway.

Out of respect to him she called him later. He was hurt and bewildered. But when she pointed out to him that because of her pregnancy she couldn't risk living in such a strained environment, he reluctantly backed off, promising that he wouldn't pressure her.

Nickie quit Stellar Attractions and returned to her old job at Hawkins and Cunningham. Then at less than three months of pregnancy, she lost the baby. The onslaught of her miscarriage was sudden; she practically collapsed with the pain at work. An associate rushed her to the hospital, and Nickie's mother and her sister, Meredith, met her there.

Jason was at a dinner business meeting when his office managed to reach him. He met Nickie in the corridor at the hospital, just as the nurses were wheeling her toward surgery.

"Nickie, I'm so sorry," he said, clutching her hand.

"I've lost the baby," she told him, sobbing heartbrokenly.

"I know, darling. We'll have another one. I love you so much."

"I love you, too."

Then, as the nurses stopped the gurney just outside the doors to surgery, Jason embraced her, and Nickie smelled the nauseating scent of Tracy Wright's custom-mixed perfume on his shirt. Everything she felt for him seemed to die in that moment—to die with the child they had already lost.

The next time Jason heard from her, it was through her attorney.

A BANGING AT THE DOOR wrenched Nickie back to the present. Shaken rudely from her memories, she wiped her tears and set down her snifter of brandy.

A sense of déjà vu gripped her as she walked to the door. Her heart pounded as she opened it.

Of course. She should have known.

Jason.

4

NICKIE CAUGHT HER BREATH in a stinging gasp and stared at Jason, mesmerized. He stood there gazing back at her, looking every bit as tall and handsome as she remembered. Yesterday became today before her very eyes. It was as if the time they'd been apart had ceased to exist, so real were her feelings—so raw her pain, so devastating the impact of his presence.

Somehow she found her voice. "What are you doing here?"

"I had an idea you might come here," he replied awkwardly. "May I come in?"

"Would it make a difference if I said no?" she asked bitterly.

"It would," he said.

Standing there in the shadows of her porch, he looked lost and vulnerable, not at all the self-possessed man she remembered. Nickie found she couldn't just slam the door in his face—as much as he deserved it.

She shrugged with a bravado she hardly felt. "Come on in."

Jason moved through the doorway, and even as she stiffened, he leaned over and kissed her cheek. It was a brief, chaste peck, but it sent her senses reeling nonetheless. Then he swept past her—filling her lungs with his spicy masculine scent, filling the room with his towering presence. He paused before the fire, warming his hands over the flames. She noted that he still wore his wedding ring. The sight of the gold band brought a lump to her throat—her rings were in her jewelry box at home.

He turned to smile at her. "I see you've built a fire. It feels nice, Nickie."

"Thanks."

"You're looking good, babe," he added softly.

At first Nickie couldn't reply as she fought the treacherous softening his smile and his husky words sent flooding through her. Her heart pounded and her cheek still burned where his lips had brushed it.

Then righteous anger rose up in her. This man had ruined her life, she reminded herself grimly. She squared her shoulders and bolstered her courage. Again she demanded, "Why are you here, Jason?"

"Don't you know?" His words hung in the electric silence, interrupted only by the roar of the surf behind her and the crackle of the fire. At last she remembered to turn and close the door. Very aware of Jason's purpose, she was grateful for the distraction and, as always, doubting her own will to fight him.

She moved awkwardly toward the coffee table and picked up her snifter of brandy. "Would you like a drink, Jason?"

"No, thanks," he said. "Actually, I haven't touched a drop since—since the day we lost our child. But you go ahead." His expression softened, becoming kindly, concerned. "You're looking a bit pale, Nickie. Perhaps you need it."

Perhaps she needed it. She glanced away quickly, her fingers trembling on the stem of her snifter. Ah, yes, she did need this drink. She was hard-pressed not to fall apart, just being in the same room with Jason Stellar again. She had almost forgotten how his presence alone could turn her inside out emotionally. Studying him covertly as he continued to warm his hands in front of the flames, she reflected that no man should be as handsome as he was. He wore a ski sweater that showcased his broad shoulders and muscular torso, and snug jeans that outlined every nerve and sinew of his long legs—every inch of his blatant masculinity. She almost groaned aloud. He had aged slightly since she'd last seen him—at thirty-two, he'd acquired slight touches of gray at his temples and the lines about his mouth had deepened. The nine-month separation had been hard on him, too, she realized with a feeling akin to compassion. On the other hand, the slight maturing of his countenance only added to his appeal, making him seem more formidable than ever.

With an effort, Nickie tore her gaze from him and took a gulp of brandy that almost choked her. Even fortified by the alcohol, she felt her knees threaten to give out; she desperately backed up to the couch and sat down.

"To what do I owe the pleasure?" she finally asked.

He turned to face her. "Nickie, I decided it was high time we met in person. I came here to get something straight with you."

"Oh?"

"I never slept with Tracy Wright."

Nickie slammed her snifter down on the coffee table, almost cracking the delicate glass. "Give me a break, Jason. You came to the hospital reeking of Tracy's perfume. I was lying there...losing your baby...and when I smelled your shirt...and saw the look in your eyes..." She stared down at her trembling hands, fighting back the tears.

Suddenly Jason was beside her, grasping her hands, the heat of his grip flowing through her. She couldn't pull away; she couldn't even trust herself to move or speak.

"Remember that time when I caught you with Hank Houston?" Jason asked at last.

She gazed defiantly at him, and wrenched her hands away. "Hank Stetson. And you didn't catch me. All I was doing was entertaining a client for lunch—"

"Wrong. You later admitted that you were thinking of doing more."

Nickie glanced away guiltily. "Jason, we weren't even married then. I was—trying to break away from you. And, furthermore, I didn't do anything. *You* did."

"Wrong again," he denied vehemently. "I did nothing with Tracy. But if I did feel guilty, it was because, well, like you, I felt . . . tempted."

He cleared his throat and continued, "That night, Tracy went with me to the dinner meeting with several of my Galleria staff. We were planning our spring show. And—Lord, I was just feeling so low, Nickie, so blue. Just weeks before, you had walked out, and—"

"And?"

He sighed, running a hand through his hair. At last his anguished eyes met hers. "I had a lot to drink that night. After the others left, Tracy hung around and—well, she made a play for me. A big play. Then I got the call from the hospital—"

"And if the call hadn't come?" Nickie challenged.

He gestured earnestly. "I wasn't going to sleep with Tracy. In fact, I was trying my best to shake her off when I was called away."

Nickie's laugh held bitterness and disbelief. "Then why did you look so damned guilty when you met me at the hospital?"

He swallowed hard. "Look at it from my perspective. Here you were, being rushed to the hospital, losing our child, while I was thinking of . . . feeling tempted by another woman."

At once she was on her feet. "So this is your explanation?" she demanded, her hand slashing the air. "That you strayed mentally and emotionally, if not physically? Don't you know that you've just confirmed my every suspicion about you?"

Now he was standing, too. "The fact of the matter is, I didn't betray you."

"Not if we want to split hairs about it."

He held out both hands in entreaty. "Nickie, I was all mixed up then. Consumed by ambition, drinking way too much. I wanted so much for you and our child. I wanted everything to be perfect. I just didn't realize that in the process, I was losing you both."

She stared at the rug. "I guess that sometimes, we all realize these things much too late."

He drew a step closer. "Won't you give us another chance?" he asked plaintively.

"No." She trembled and blinked back hot tears. "I don't have another heart left to break."

His entreaty continued as he moved toward her. "But I won't break your heart this time. I've worked out a lot of things since we've been apart. I'm more settled now. I don't have to travel as much, and . . . I've changed, Nickie."

Her gaze collided with his. "I wish I could believe that."

He stared down at her searchingly. "Don't you even believe me about Tracy?"

She laughed shortly. "That story is almost too ridiculous not to be true. But it doesn't change the basic fact that our marriage was—and still is—unworkable. We've just never been in the same league."

"That's a matter of opinion."

With an exasperated sigh, Nickie moved toward the fire. "Jason, when are you going to quit fighting the divorce?"

"When you give me what I want."

She whirled to face him with eyes blazing. "That's out of the question."

"Then I guess we'll just go on fighting, won't we?"

His words made something snap inside her. "How can you ask for this beach house?"

He moved toward her with that resolute gleam in his eye. "I think that would be obvious. This beach house is very special to me. We made a baby here, remember?"

Oh, did she ever! "It's *my* beach house, Jason," she exclaimed desperately.

"It used to be ours."

Nickie gazed at him in despair. She didn't know how much more of this she could take. At last she said, "Jason, we're getting nowhere with this. I think you should leave."

He closed the space between them. "Damn it, why won't you even acknowledge the possibility that I might be different now?"

She fought the stirring effect of his nearness on her. "Our worlds always were poles apart. You were too driven, I was too down-to-earth. I think I always knew in my heart that we were just not meant to be. That I wasn't the right woman for you."

"Nickie, no! You can't mean that."

She continued angrily. "I do! Face it, Jason. I've never fit into your glitzy, glamorous world. Perhaps you should be with someone like Tracy—"

"No," he insisted. "Don't you know that you're everything I've ever—"

"If I truly was what you wanted, you would have fought for me more," she cut in passionately. "But the fact of the matter is, you weren't there for me when I needed you. And then, when you did show up . . ." Her voice trailed off and she shuddered.

He laid his hand gently on her shoulder, and waited until she dared to look up at him. "Nickie, I'll be there for you this time. I promise."

She drew a long, shaky breath. "I can't risk it again. I just can't."

They fell into a strained, unhappy silence. Jason's hand dropped to his side. A log settled with a thud in the grate. Outside, the surf surged and the wind howled.

At last Jason murmured, "Tell me something."

"Yes?"

"Why did you come here?"

"What?" she asked, taken aback.

"You say we were never meant to be," he continued in a hoarse whisper, his blue eyes impaling her. "But wasn't it the memories that brought you back here tonight? The memories of you and me on that couch together?"

Oh, he'd done it now! Nickie stared at the couch—remembering, sinking, dying inside. "Jason, please stop."

But he closed in, gripping her by the shoulders. "Wasn't it the memories?"

Staring up into his tormented eyes, Nickie knew she couldn't deny his words. Not after what they had shared here. "Maybe it was," she admitted softly.

Yet even as he moved to kiss her, she pushed him away and pleaded, "Leave me my memories, Jason. Let me have something beautiful to hold on to from our marriage. Don't take even that away from me. Don't destroy it all."

For a long moment, he stared at her in pained disbelief. "It really is over for you, isn't it?"

She couldn't answer. She barely managed to nod.

"You won't give us one last chance?"

She managed to shake her head.

"All right, then, I'll go." The bitterness in his voice
seared through her.

She stared back at the fire, not daring to watch him
leave.

She heard the door whip open, felt the breeze surging
in, and then she heard his low, tortured voice once more.
"Oh, I almost forgot—I brought you something."

With a perplexed frown, Nickie turned to face him.

Shutting the door, Jason moved back toward her. A
muscle worked in his strong, square jaw as he pressed a
black savings passbook into her hand. Yet his tone was
surprisingly gentle as he said, "I wanted you to have
this."

She stared up at him, confused. "What is this?
Money?"

He nodded, and she found her heartstrings catching
at the pain she glimpsed in his eyes. He cleared his throat.
"When we found out you were pregnant, I started a college fund for our child. I just . . . felt you should have this
now."

Nickie stared from the passbook to him, tears stinging her eyes. "Why are you giving this to me now?" she
asked in a strangled whisper. "Are you trying to kill me?"

At once he shook his head, looking alarmed and genuinely contrite. "No, Nickie, no. Of course not."

"Then, why?"

He glanced away, swallowing hard, and again he wore
that lost expression that tugged so poignantly at her
emotions. "If you want to know the truth, I just didn't

know what else to do with the passbook. I didn't have the heart to close the account." He glanced back at her lamely, and for a moment they shared a look of remembered anguish. "As for remarriage—I don't think it's for me. But someday you'll marry Hank Texas, or someone, and have his baby—"

"I—don't think I can," she choked out, her fingers clenching on the passbook.

"You can," he assured her gently. "I spoke with the doctor at the hospital, and he said that what happened to you before was most likely just a fluke, that there's no reason you can't have many children."

"No, that's not what I mean. I mean that, emotionally, I can't—"

"You can," he insisted with a kind smile. "Anyway, when you do have a child, I want him—or her—to have this money."

Nickie stared at the precious folder through her tears. She felt shattered, beyond speech.

Jason leaned over and kissed her cheek. "Goodbye, Nickie."

For a long time afterward, Nickie would wonder what made her run after him, what made her grip his sleeve and say brokenly, "Jason, no. Don't go. Not like this."

He whirled, uttering a raw cry, and then she was in his arms. The passbook fluttered to the floor as they kissed each other hungrily. Wave after wave of powerful emotion assailed her as she clung to him and kissed him back.

Nickie had almost forgotten how wonderful it felt to be in Jason's arms, to have him kissing her, holding her against his pounding heart. All at once the world receded and they were just two people sharing the same remembered pain, releasing a heartache borne separately for so long. Their lost child, their shattered mar-

riage. Who better—who else—could either of them share
it with? she thought achingly.

"Nickie, I love you," Jason whispered through tears,
desperately kissing her cheek, her throat, her temple.

She stretched to kiss the firm, beloved line of his jaw.
"I know. But it's still impossible—"

"Don't say that. It's not impossible. It's not over. Lord,
babe, I missed you so much—"

"Me, too."

"I've been so lonely—"

"Me, too."

Both of them trembled as he picked her up, carried her
to the couch and pressed her down. Why had she ever
fought him? she wondered. They always ended up this
way.

He did little more than unzip his jeans and her slacks,
then he was inside her, thrusting deep, and she reeled
with ecstasy, feeling as if she'd come home after a long
absence. She pulled her sweater high and brought his
head down to her breast. He sucked at her nipple through
the wispy lace of her bra and she lost control, ripping at
the front closure, pressing her bare breast deeply into the
wonderful heat of his mouth. Her hungry hands yanked
up his sweater and shirt; her fingernails dug into the
silken texture of his back. Then her voracious lips demanded his again, her tongue plunging and colliding
with his, tasting the well-remembered texture of his
mouth.

"Oh, Nickie." As he groaned and buried his lips
against the throbbing pulse in her throat, she caught her
breath in sharp gasps and ran her fingers wildly through
his hair. He pressed harder and she clenched about him,
the hot, straining pressure of him driving her toward a
sweet violence of sensation. She felt herself climaxing

with an intensity she'd never known before, giving herself over totally to the moment and their love. They devoured each other; they mated.

Afterward, for long, languorous moments, they lay still joined. Then reality crashed in on Nickie. She tried to push him away. "Oh, Lord, Jason, what have we done? We didn't—"

"Don't get up," he begged gently, his eyes entreating her, his features burnished gold by the flickering firelight. "Don't wash away our lovemaking. Stay here with me tonight. Please, Nickie, I need you so."

"Oh, Jason."

When he kissed her again, she was lost.

After the second time they made love, she didn't want to move.

After the third time, she couldn't.

THE HARDEST THING Nickie ever did was to get up the next morning and face Jason. Nine o'clock found the two of them in the cramped little kitchen. Jason sat at the small table, silently watching Nickie as she moved about in her robe, preparing coffee.

Nickie's hands trembled as she loaded the coffee maker and turned it on. There was no way she could escape the reality of their lovemaking last night—indeed, her body wouldn't let her. She hadn't made love with Jason—or with anyone, for that matter—for almost a year, and they had devoured each other voraciously all night. Now, every movement brought twinges of carnal memory.

And the fact that Jason had come to the table unshaven and wearing only his well-fitting jeans, didn't help matters at all! Nickie eyed him resentfully as she pulled two cups down from the cupboard. With his rumpled hair and muscular chest, he looked sexy enough to devour on the spot. And he was staring back at her with a familiar animal gleam in his eye.

Even more shattering had been Jason's words of love the night before. She dared not believe him, not now when she was struggling for her own emotional survival. Surely they'd both just been caught up in the passion of the moment, in the devastating sexual and emotional pull that refused to die out with the rest of their marriage.

Nickie approached the table with two filled cups. Setting them down and taking her seat, she managed to say primly, "You might at least have put on your shirt, Jason."

"What?" He laughed, his eyes suddenly dancing with mischief. "And this from the girl who practically strangled me pulling it off last night?"

Nickie lifted her coffee cup to hide her acute discomfort. "Aren't you cold?"

"Actually, baby, I'm still trying to cool off."

Nickie's cup clattered to the table.

Jason reached across the table and took her hand. "Hey, hon, lighten up a bit. I would think that last night changes things."

"You would," she said resentfully. "But it doesn't for me."

"Then what was last night?" he exclaimed. "Were you just hard up, Nickie?"

"Certainly not," she replied, her cheeks flaming.

He was silent for a long moment. "You know, it wasn't until I met you that I feared a woman might want me just for sex."

Nickie stared up at him in amazement. She'd so often had that very same kind of doubt about him. "You're kidding!"

"Hell, no," he growled. "Do you think women are the only ones who fear they might be used as a sex object?"

"Well, I . . ." Nickie raked a hand through her tousled hair. She desperately wanted *not* to be having this conversation with Jason right now! She couldn't repress a hint of a smile as she murmured, "I guess, when you have a package as attractive as yours . . ."

"Well, that's just great, Nickie. So damned comforting and reassuring." He leaned back in his chair and crossed his tanned, muscular arms over his chest. "But you're still not going to weasel out of this."

"Weasel out of what?"

"So tell me, what exactly did last night mean to you? Was it just a passing weakness on your part—a momentary lapse?"

She sighed. "Jason, of course there's some feeling left between us. The chemistry between us was always—"

"Explosive?"

Her fingers clutched the edge of the tabletop. "Yes. But it's just not enough to base a marriage on."

He slammed his fist on the tabletop, making her jump, rattling the coffee cups. "Nickie, why won't you give us another chance? I've changed."

"You keep saying that," she acknowledged miserably. "But you have to realize something, Jason. Everything that happened between us before hurt me so much. It's been hell recovering my equilibrium, getting my life back in order again. I just don't think I can risk it another time."

"It seems to me you risked a hell of a lot more than that, last night."

"And you had nothing to do with that, right?"

"Who followed me to the door?" he challenged.

"And who gave me the bankbook?" Fresh tears stung her eyes. "Don't you know you practically killed me with that?"

Even as she tried to recoil, he grasped both of her hands in his and said earnestly, "Darling, I didn't mean the gesture to hurt you. I just wanted you to have—"

"I know." Fighting her treacherous response to him, she lifted her chin. "Still—you came here to seduce me, didn't you?"

"No," he denied. "I came here to explain about Tracy. After you left me, you wouldn't even listen to me. Then everything was through the lawyers. If you'd just come to me—hell, I might have given you the divorce."

She tossed her head. "That's a laugh. After last night, I wouldn't believe it in a million years."

He leaned toward her intently. "Nickie, I didn't come here to seduce you." He reached out and stroked her cheek, and his tone held a devastating, husky note as he added, "But I will admit this: The minute I laid eyes on you, I knew I wanted to."

"No fair," she pleaded, melting beneath the heat of his scrutiny. "It's always too easy for you."

"Think how much easier it would be to give in and come home with me," he said tenderly.

"No." She shuddered. "You'd swallow me up."

He smiled. "I'd certainly try to. Just think, darling— we could have another baby."

"I don't want your baby," she said shakily.

"You do. You just won't admit it."

Fighting to hold on to herself, Nickie got up and began to pace. "Why are you doing this to me?"

He stared at her incredulously. "Isn't it obvious by now? I want you back, of course."

"Why?" she demanded.

"Why?" He appeared flabbergasted. "Why do you think I married you in the first place?"

She continued to pace the narrow galley. "I really have no idea," she said, waving a hand. "Maybe you thought we made a good team. Or maybe it was because you were my first, and you felt duty-bound to do the old-fashioned, honorable thing. Maybe now you're hanging on to our marriage out of guilt—"

He surged to his feet. "Guilt? That's the biggest bunch of crap I've ever heard. What have you been doing, anyway? Reading dime-store books on marriage analysis?"

She stopped in her tracks to face him. "Well, I can't help it. It's just the way I feel. Especially after everything that happened." She drew a deep, shuddering breath. "How many ways can I say this? It's over."

"You can say that after last night?"

"Yes."

He drew a step closer. "What if— I mean, what if after last night, you're already—"

Realization dawned on Nickie, and her eyes widened. "So that's what last night was about!"

"No! You must know I'd never—"

She held up a hand. "Look, let's not worry about that right now. I don't think I can handle it just yet."

He nodded. "Okay. But, you know, there's a simple solution to all of this."

"Oh?"

"I still want a trial reconciliation," he said earnestly.

Nickie shook her head and stared at the ceiling. She was exhausted. She felt as if she'd been standing at the edge of the beach all night, single-handedly trying to hold the tide at bay. "Oh, Jason, have I been talking to the four walls all morning? What am I going to do with you?"

He crossed the distance between them and took her in his arms. She shivered as his stirring nearness played havoc with her senses, her resolve. Memories of their beautiful lovemaking slammed her remorselessly as his heat seeped into her and his scent filled her lungs.

"Are you really fishing for suggestions?" he asked tenderly.

All at once, Nickie had to laugh. He sounded just like the old Jason. Indeed, the whole encounter seemed straight out of their past—their heated spats, and the way that afterward, they'd... Steering her thoughts away from dangerous territory, she twisted in his arms to stare up at him.

Jason stroked her temple with his fingertips. "So last night changes nothing for you?" he asked, again with surprising gentleness. "Can you honestly say that?"

"No," she admitted, resting her cheek against his chest, feeling strangely comforted by the steady thud of his heart in her ear. Suddenly he seemed like an old friend she was sharing her troubles with. They had been such good friends—once.

"Well, then?"

She sighed deeply. "I can't decide anything right now. I'm too confused."

His gaze held joy and new hope. "But you are willing to consider the possibility of giving us another chance?"

"I guess—after last night—I'd be a hypocrite if I didn't reconsider things."

He stared down into her eyes. "When?"

"Give me some time, Jason. A few weeks. I've got to think this through."

He grinned. "Okay, then. But you'll let me know if—"

She emitted a small, strangled sound. "Yes, I'll let you know."

He moved to kiss her, but she pressed her hands against his chest. "Jason, I really need the time. Beginning now."

"Sure, Nickie."

But before she could protest, he pulled her up hard against him and claimed her lips in a long, searing, enervating kiss. Then, whistling as he grabbed his things from the living room, he was gone.

In the kitchen, Nickie reeled. She wondered if she'd lost her mind.

TIME. For ten agonizing days, Nickie waited to see if she was pregnant. She waited with a sense of dread, a sense of wonder. She felt reasonably confident that their timing had been off that night at the beach house, but she couldn't be sure.

She knew that if she was pregnant, there was absolutely no question of abortion. She could never even consider that option after losing her baby last year. Nor was there any question of her wanting to wipe out any lasting manifestation of her and Jason's beautiful, reckless night together. It would be like saying their love had never existed.

Most disconcerting of all was the fact that if she was pregnant, she knew she'd be tempted to give Jason another chance, for the baby's sake. And for hers, too, she had to admit. Jason had said he'd changed. He'd said he still loved her. If only she could believe him!

On the tenth morning, she awakened to the discovery that she wouldn't have his child. She felt the barest flicker of relief, and then she was off to the bathroom, where she wept irrationally for nearly an hour.

It was then that she realized that her not being pregnant hadn't really changed anything. She was still tempted to give Jason another chance. After what had happened between them at the beach house, her resolve was terribly shaken. In spite of her lingering doubts about being the right woman for him, she had to acknowledge that she had missed him, and that she might still love him.

She called him and invited him to meet her on Sunday afternoon at Memorial Park. On that crisp mid-November day, she arrived early, and tried to build up her courage as she waited for him near the trail where they used to jog. Still, her heart thumped wildly as she watched him approach wearing jeans and a leather jacket. He looked tense, expectant—and more devastatingly handsome than ever in his stylish dark glasses, with the breeze whipping through his thick, shiny hair.

He pecked her cheek, eyeing her appreciatively. Her pulse quickened as he took her hand and they started down the familiar trail.

For a few moments they walked quietly through the fragrant pines. "Well?" he asked at last.

"I'm not pregnant," she said.

His reaction was anything but what she had anticipated. She had expected him to curse his own disappointment, but instead he took off his glasses and studied her intently, sympathetically. "Are you disappointed, darling?"

"I think the timing would have been poor," she said awkwardly.

"Perhaps so." They walked on for a moment. Then he sighed and asked, "Why did you ask me here today, Nickie? Have you thought things through, as you said you would?"

"I have." She took a deep breath, then met his gaze. "Jason, about the divorce..."

"Yes?"

"You're still going to fight it to the death, aren't you?"

He smiled. "Yes."

"What if I give you the trial reconciliation?" At the look of naked joy in his eyes, she held up a hand. "On my terms."

"Terms? But first tell me, what changed your mind? Was it the beach house?"

She glanced away, acutely embarrassed.

"It was our lovemaking, wasn't it?" he prompted.

Avoiding his prodding, she warned, "Jason, I'm not promising this will be permanent."

"Okay, darling. Then tell me about your terms."

She bit her lip. "Three months. Until spring."

"That's reasonable."

"After that, if I still don't think our marriage can work, we'll divorce quietly. Out of court. No more contesting on your part—not over anything."

He shrugged. "Okay."

"I want your promise on that, Jason."

"All right, I promise."

"During the next three months, I'll see you—twice a week."

"Three times."

"Okay, three times. But I won't live with you."

He raised an eyebrow at that.

"Jason, it's either my way or not at all."

"Okay. You won't live with me. Go on."

"And I won't sleep with you."

There, he grinned.

She waved her forefinger at him. "Jason Stellar, so help me, if you try to force things—"

He held up both hands in a gesture of feigned innocence. "Nickie, you know damned well that I've never used force with you. And I'm not about to start now."

"Just so you understand. There are too many other issues we need to resolve first."

"I understand. And you've got a deal, Nickie Stellar." But, again, he grinned—that infuriating, confident grin.

"Damn it, Jason, I'm not going to sleep with you," she gritted out.

He reached out and just grazed her cheek with his fingertips. His voice rolled over her like a silken caress. "Famous last words, darling."

5

A FEW DAYS LATER, Jason's mind was very much on Nickie as he maneuvered his car through the maze of early-morning Houston traffic. He smiled as he recalled the previous two weeks. He and Nickie had made a lot of progress in their relationship—especially that emotional night at the beach house, when she had let down her guard and come into his arms again. His heart pounded as he remembered the heaven of making love to her and holding her close all night once more. Now she was willing to give them another chance.

If only he didn't blow it!

He certainly had his work cut out for him in winning her back. He recalled the doubts she had expressed at the beach house—that perhaps he'd married her out of some sense of duty, or because he'd felt they made a good team—and he wondered why she was so convinced that she was wrong for him.

To Jason, Nickie had always been the right woman for him. She'd been his stability, his oasis, in a hectic, uncertain world. He had always felt that they complemented each other perfectly—her down-to-earth, sensible qualities balancing out his more mercurial, hard-driving nature. How could he convince her that he wanted *her*? Her conduct at the beach house certainly demonstrated that she still doubted his feelings. Now he feared that if he simply told her what was in his heart, she would turn a deaf ear. He also suspected that she was going along with the reconciliation largely because she knew she'd get her divorce in the end. She just wasn't ready to trust him yet—and he could understand her doubts. They had a lot of rebuilding to do before she would be ready to hear and believe his feelings.

Still, the dilemma remained: how to win her back? He thought of the days when they'd first met, remembering how they'd grown closer through working together in his business. Perhaps he should try to go back to their beginnings, and get it right this time....

Jason continued to brood as he drove into the parking garage, then took the elevator up to his corporate headquarters. As soon as he was in his office and settled behind his desk, he picked up the phone and dialed Nickie's number at Hawkins and Cunningham. "Good morning, darling."

"Oh, hi, Jason," she replied cautiously.

"You busy right now?"

"I've got a client coming in a few minutes."

"This won't take long. How've you been?"

"Fine."

He scowled to himself. She sounded annoyed. "Something wrong?"

"I'm just rather surprised...."

Jason was intrigued by the note of petulance he heard in her voice. "By what?"

"Well, after you made such a big deal of saying you had to see me three times a week, you've waited four days to call me."

"So you've been counting the days until you heard from me again, have you, Nickie?"

"Certainly not!" she retorted. "I'm just rather surprised that—er—after you insisted— Oh, never mind!"

"Just trying to keep you off balance, sweetheart."

"Well, don't hold your breath."

"Actually, I had to make a quick trip to Dallas and San Antonio to check on our stores there," he explained. "You know how it is when we're in the middle of the Christmas season."

"Right." She paused a moment. "So why are you calling, Jason?"

"I have a proposition for you."

She harrumphed. "Perhaps I should summon my attorneys."

"No, it's nothing like that. I was just wondering if you'd like to accompany me to Galveston on Saturday."

"To Galveston?"

"I've been eyeballing a choice rental there, not far from the Strand. I'm thinking of starting another store down on the island."

Nickie whistled. "A seventh store? Aren't six enough for you?"

He chuckled. "You know my business philosophy. Grow or stagnate. Anyway, I'd love to have you come with me and look at the rental. I'd really value your opinion."

Nickie was cautiously quiet for a long moment. At last she said, "Jason, I just don't think it would be wise for me to get involved in your business again. Besides, I'm getting pretty busy myself here at work, with tax time approaching and annual budgets being due."

"Nickie, I'm not asking you for any kind of long-term commitment to this venture, nor would I try to take you away from your other duties. It's just that I'd like to know what you think at this initial stage." A whimsical note entered his voice. "And I guess I've also been remembering the fun we used to have traveling around the state, scouting various locations for my new stores."

On the other end, Nickie couldn't resist a smile as she, too, recalled those earlier, happier days. "Yes, we did have fun. Still, why are you considering a Galveston store? I would think that the market there would be marginal at best."

"Galveston does draw a strong tourist trade. And besides, I *have* to have this store."

Nickie felt alarmed by a note of near desperation she heard in his voice. "You *have* to have this store? Jason, if you're overextended, then going further out on a limb isn't the answer."

He chuckled again. "Sounds to me like my business—and perhaps more than my business—is still very much in your blood."

"I played an active role in helping your business expand, so of course I still feel some sense of interest and commitment," she said defensively. "And, besides, I'd hate to see you ruin it all now—and wreck my prospects in divorce court."

He laughed. "What a heartwarming attitude. Those being your sentiments, you'll come with me on Saturday?"

"Yes, but just this once."

"I'll be happy to pay you a consulting fee."

"Don't be ridiculous. I'll be happy to offer you an opinion—as a friend."

"As a friend," he repeated. A husky note crept into his voice. "Well, if that's all you're willing to give me at this point, Nickie Stellar, then I'll have to be content with it. However, maybe we can work on turning that word *friend* into *lover*."

"Only if—and when—it's my idea," Nickie insisted, over her pounding heart.

"Darling, it will be my pleasure to persuade you that it's your idea," Jason said.

NICKIE COULDN'T RESIST a smile as she leaned back in her leather chair. She realized that Jason had been right—she *had* been counting the days until she heard from him again, and she'd been thrilled to hear his voice just now. She was even more delighted that she'd be seeing him again soon.

Yet she frowned as she thought of the purpose of the date they'd made for Saturday. Jason had claimed he had changed, yet here he was charging ahead again, planning a seventh store in Galveston. And the fact that he was asking for her business advice did little to assuage her doubts, either. Then again, she wondered if he was pursuing her in part because he wanted to get a successful team back together. She feared he might be in financial trouble, and wanted her advice to help him regain stability.

Had she made a mistake in agreeing to this trial reconciliation? She sighed. Whether she had been foolish or not, she had made the commitment, and she was not a person to break her promises. Besides, she was well aware that seeing Jason again was the only way she could get him to quit fighting the divorce.

Still, she felt more than a little vulnerable as she recalled his promise to take them from being friends to being lovers again.

She knew she had placed herself in the hands of a man perfectly capable of charming and seducing her; of turning her emotions and her resolve into chaos.

SATURDAY NICKIE AWOKE early, filled with excitement and anticipation. She took special pains with her appearance. As she stood in the bathroom in her underwear and slip, putting on her makeup at the mirror, she mused that she was as nervous as a schoolgirl before her first date.

Once she had finished with her toilette, she glanced at her reflection and sighed. The shower had given her skin a fresh, rosy glow, her dark hair gleamed, and the makeup she had scrupulously applied highlighted her rounded cheekbones, full mouth and dark eyes. Still, her face seemed plain, interesting only in a pixieish sort of way. She knew she would never be beautiful; even "pretty" seemed a stretch. Ruefully she glanced down at her small, reedy body. Even wearing a black slip, she hardly looked like a femme fatale, but rather, exactly like what she was: a skinny person masquerading in sexy black lingerie. She wondered for the thousandth time what Jason saw in her. Finished dressing, she was about to shut her jewelry case when she glanced poignantly at her wedding rings and was tempted to put them on. Tears clouded her eyes for a moment as she thought of how Jason tenaciously still wore his wedding band.

Then she quickly snapped the case shut. She wouldn't, *couldn't* don those rings again until the day she felt completely committed to Jason. She wasn't sure if that day would come.

She caught a last glimpse of herself in the bedroom mirror. "You've done your best, kid," she murmured, eyeing her blue cashmere sweater and short black wool skirt. Splashing on a bit of her favorite perfume, she couldn't help but feel rather pleased by her appearance.

Jason was early. He looked at her and whistled. "Good morning, Nickie. You look great!"

"Thanks," she murmured, pleased by his approval. "Why don't you come in for a minute while I finish up in the kitchen and grab my purse?"

"Sure."

Inside Nickie's town house, Jason followed her to the kitchen. She caught a whiff of his enticing cologne and began questioning her sanity for agreeing to see him today. He looked—and smelled—good enough to eat on the spot. Still, vanity forced her to wonder whether he would notice the perfume she wore—his favorite, of course; the very brand he'd once dabbed all over her as they lay in bed....

"You smell good, Nickie," he murmured, as if he'd read her thoughts.

She glanced up at him, blushing, feeling disarmed by the look of tender amusement in his eyes. "You remembered."

"Of course, I remembered."

"You do know how to choose a perfume, Jason."

"And a wife," he added meaningfully. "Why'd you wear the perfume, Nickie? Because of me?"

She shrugged with bravado. "Because I like it."

He smiled and touched her arm, effectively restraining her efforts as his fingers slid up and down her sleeve all too caressingly. "I like this sweater—it's soft, feminine, like you."

Even through the heavy sweater, his touch sent goose bumps up her arms and a shiver down her spine, and his seductive words were equally unsettling. Her eyes kept straying to his beautifully shaped hand—the long, tanned fingers and neatly manicured nails. Jason's hands used to touch her in ways that had made her climb the walls, she recalled. Now his touch aroused potent sensual memories in every part of her—

Abruptly the phone rang, shattering her sexual fantasizing. "Hello?" she answered tensely, still very aware of Jason's heated gaze on her.

To her dismay, Nickie heard Jim McMurray's voice on
the other end. "Hi, Nickie. How are you doing?" he began.

Nickie felt a sharp stab of guilt that she'd been avoiding Jim this past week; she still hadn't had a chance to tell
him that she and Jason were seeing each other again.

"Oh, hi, Jim. How are you?" she replied awkwardly,
aware of Jason's glower.

"I was wondering if you might have some free time this
weekend," Jim continued. "I meant to make a date with
you at work, but you know how harried we've all been
lately. Anyway, how about dinner—perhaps tonight or
tomorrow?"

Hating the fact that she had to have this conversation
in front of Jason, Nickie said, "I'm sorry, Jim, but I just
can't see you this weekend." Turning away from Jason,
she lowered her voice and continued, "Look, I really
can't talk right now, but there are some things we need
to discuss. Can we get together some time next week?
Perhaps lunch..." As he responded in the affirmative,
she quickly finished, "Okay, then, we'll arrange something at work. Bye."

"So, you haven't told Jim that you and I are back together?" Jason demanded angrily.

Nickie met Jason's hard, glittering gaze. "We're not
back together, Jason."

He crossed his arms over his chest. "Oh, we're not?"

She nervously ran a hand through her hair. "I
just...haven't had a chance to tell Jim what's going on."

"So, what is going on, Nickie? I'd really like to know."

Nickie resisted the urge to get into a full-scale argument with him. Spotting her purse on the countertop
near the canisters, she grabbed it and asked, "You
ready?"

"Of course," he said with biting sarcasm. "It's you—and darling Jim—who have kept us waiting."

The atmosphere was strained between them as they went out the front door. Jason strode along in moody silence as they went to his car. He managed to usher Nickie into the Mercedes without even touching her. She fastened her safety belt and sighed unhappily as she watched him walk around to his side. Then he was beside her, slamming the door, putting on his dark glasses and turning the key.

"So how's your week been?" he asked with strained courtesy as they pulled away from the curb.

"Okay, if busy. Actually, I'm looking forward to the Christmas holidays next month—we're shutting down for a week."

"That will be a nice break for you," he agreed. Pointedly he added, "And I do hope you'll be reserving a good deal of that time for me."

Nickie turned to stare out the window. She regretted her slip about the holidays—there was something so intimate about spending Christmas with someone, and she wasn't sure she was ready for that kind of intimacy with Jason again.

Jason cleared his throat noisily. "Nickie, about what just happened . . ."

She turned to him, feeling her hackles rising. "Yes?"

"Don't you think that if we're going to give this marriage another chance, we shouldn't be seeing other people?"

Nickie bristled. How dare he practically accuse her of cheating, when he was the one who'd had the roving eye during their marriage! Hadn't he recently admitted that he'd felt tempted by Tracy Wright? "Jason, I'm going to have lunch with Jim next week because I owe him an explanation. We did date casually for a while, and I should tell him that things have—changed."

Jason uttered a deprecating growl as he accelerated the car. "Perhaps you'd like to string him along for a while, in case things don't work out with me."

Nickie's jaw dropped and she blinked in angry disbelief. "Of all the— That's really low, Jason!"

Jason gripped the steering wheel tightly. "Okay, maybe I'm overreacting," he admitted at last. "But when we made our agreement, we didn't bring up dating other people, and—"

"Look," she cut in, "when I agreed to this trial reconciliation, the fact that I wouldn't become involved with other men was something I considered to be a foregone conclusion. But knowing you, I'm not surprised that you feel we have to spell everything out."

"Would you believe me, Nickie, if I told you I haven't slept with anyone else since we broke up?"

She considered this with a deep frown. "No."

He uttered a vivid curse. "Nickie, all I'm trying to say is that we shouldn't let other people cloud the issues during this trial period. I'm talking about the entire emotional gamut of our relationship—sex, too."

As much as his reference to the physical side of their relationship stirred a treacherous softening in her, she managed to grit her teeth and reply, "Jason, I've told you repeatedly that I'm not promising this will work—nor will I promise that I'll sleep with you again."

"I realize that. I'm just saying that if we do sleep with anyone during this period, it should be with each other. And I think we should make that a ground rule."

She sniffed. "And I still contend that your 'ground rule' should go without saying."

"Nickie?" he urged reproachfully.

Exasperated, she exclaimed, "All right, I'll agree—if you'll agree to think about taking your own advice."

6

THE LONG DRIVE to Galveston—passed mostly in silence—gave them an opportunity to cool off. Nickie spent the first half-hour seething. The gall of him, insinuating that she might sleep with another man while still married to him!

But as she calmed down, she was able to see things from his perspective. Jim McMurray's phone call had been unfortunate, but it had also been largely her fault; she really should have told Jim last week that her divorce had been put on hold. And she knew that if she'd been at Jason's condo and some woman he'd been dating had phoned him, she would have been livid.

Spending Christmas with Jason was another matter. It had been just before Christmas, when she'd been fourteen, that her father had walked out. Nonetheless, Nickie, her brother, Mack, and her older sister, Meredith, had all tried their best to cheer up their very depressed mother. On Christmas Eve, they'd gathered to decorate the tree. Things had gone well at first, until her mother had pulled a particular ornament out of the box, glanced at it briefly, and then rushed from the room in tears.

Nickie had picked up the ornament her mother had dropped on the rug. It was a sterling-silver bell, inscribed with, "To Vivian. Love, Malcolm." As she had stood there holding the bell with trembling fingers, Nickie had seethed in outrage. She'd recalled her father giving the ornament to her mother the previous Christmas, and the hypocrisy of his act rankled; Nickie had realized that her dad must have been cheating on her mom even then.

But despite his betrayal, Nickie had adored her handsome, charming father. She'd also lost him at a very sensitive, vulnerable age, and she had missed him, despite the anger she felt on her mother's behalf. Yet the pain of his desertion had taught her an important lesson: that captivating men could also be liars and cheats, and that they just might not stick around for a lifetime....

Nickie glanced at Jason, looking so handsome and so tense. Was she subconsciously distrustful of Jason because of her father's desertion? Perhaps. Like her father, Jason hadn't been there when she'd needed him, that night she'd lost their child. She would give Jason another chance, but she couldn't forget the past.

JASON, TOO, was immersed in thought as they followed the interstate. He realized he'd gotten off on the wrong foot with Nickie this morning—but, damn it, she'd been standing right there in front of him, brazenly flirting with her boyfriend on the phone. She was his *wife*, and there was no way he was going to let her see someone else right now. Nickie was far from being truly his again, but the thought of her being with another man was pure torture. At least they'd gotten things straight then and there—even if it had made her angry and defensive.

How could he break through her resistance and mistrust? He'd been itching to take her into his arms all morning, even though he knew that the timing was wrong. In fact, right now, he wanted nothing more than to suggest they check into a hotel for the weekend. He knew that sex wasn't the answer to everything, but it did have a way of tearing down the barriers. He wanted to be deep inside her and look into her eyes and make her believe in him.

APPROACHING GALVESTON, they took the causeway over the gleaming blue bay that separated the island from the Texas mainland. The freeway ended shortly thereafter, and they angled onto historic Broadway, with its shady, palm-tree-dotted esplanades. Traffic was light on this off-season day, and since the weather was mild, Nickie rolled down her window and took deep breaths of the crisp, salty air.

Jason turned off toward downtown, taking them through the East End Historical District. Nickie drank in the passing sights—stately old churches and fascinating homes ranging from charming turn-of-the-century cottages to extravagant Greek Revival and Victorian mansions. Once they reached the central business district, they parked on the Strand not far from the visitors' center, then strolled down the sidewalk of the street named after the famous Strand in London, England. Both Jason and Nickie were enthralled by the elegant gaslights and century-old structures lining the quaint thoroughfare.

"Where is the rental you want to see?" Nickie asked Jason.

"It's around the block, not far from the Tremont Hotel," he replied. "But I thought we'd have an early lunch first—if that's okay with you."

"Sure."

They went into the elegant Wentletrap, admiring the antique wooden bar and the soaring ceilings.

When a waiter came to take their drink orders, Nickie was pleasantly surprised when Jason requested a Perrier water rather than his usual white wine or Scotch.

"You really aren't drinking these days, are you, Jason?" she asked after the waiter went off.

He shook his head gravely. "I meant what I said at the beach house, Nickie. I haven't touched a drop since the day we broke up."

They were both quiet for a moment, each privately remembering that painful time. After the waiter set down their drinks, Nickie said, "I'm curious—what made you decide to give up booze?"

He was preoccupied, squeezing lime into his Perrier. "Oh, a variety of reasons. Alcohol had obviously become a problem in our marriage—and an even bigger problem for me, personally. Considering my family history, I thought it best to get a handle on the situation before I risked going the route my dad did."

She nodded. "I remember your mentioning that he had a drinking problem. So that spurred you to quit?"

"In part. Alcoholism does run in families."

"Was it hard?

He laughed. "Difficult enough that I went to a few counseling sessions."

"You're kidding!" As he raised an eyebrow at her, she added quickly, "I see that you're not. Did the counseling help? I mean, if you don't mind talking about it."

"I don't." Yet his expression mirrored a struggle of emotions as he leaned back in his chair. "I suppose I learned that I'm more like my father than I care to admit. That's ironic, since the last thing I ever wanted was to be like him."

"Like him? In what ways?"

"Oh, the obsessive ambitions, the drinking..." He sighed. "Growing up, I watched alcohol destroy my parents' marriage—and wreck my father's health. It's not a process I'd particularly care to repeat."

She stared at him compassionately. "Your dad died pretty young, didn't he?"

Jason nodded grimly. "At fifty-five. The doctor said that if the smoking and drinking hadn't gotten to his heart first, cirrhosis would surely have killed him in another year or so. I remember him and my mom fighting after one of his checkups—my mom screaming at him because of his enlarged liver and my dad walking straight out and getting drunk again."

"I'm sorry, Jason." She frowned. "But didn't you once say your mother always stood by him?"

He laughed bitterly. "She stayed in the marriage, if that's what you mean. But she was a martyr every step of the way. Sometimes I think it would have been far better if she had walked out."

"Oh, I'm not so sure, Jason," Nickie said, her eyes glistening with anguish as she remembered her earlier thoughts in the car. "My dad walked out with another woman while the three of us kids were still in high school. It was a crushing blow to all of us—but particularly to my mom."

"I remember you telling me about it," he said sympathetically. He reached across the table and took her hand, his gaze meeting hers earnestly. "You know, considering our similar backgrounds, you'd think we'd both be determined to make this marriage work."

"You have a point," Nickie agreed. "Still, sometimes I think the idea of a truly happy marriage is just a myth." Watching him frown and withdraw his hand, she quickly added, "But I am glad you made the decision to give up alcohol mostly for your own sake. It seems that a major change like that has to come from inside to be really effective, and it shows a lot of maturity on your part."

He smiled. "I did learn a lot about myself in the process. And I'm glad you seem to recognize that I'm capable of changing—and growing."

"Perhaps in some ways," she said cautiously.

He scowled at that, but further discussion was cut short when the waiter returned to take their lunch orders.

Nickie realized that their long talk had relieved some of the tension between them and had also made her feel closer to Jason. The admissions he'd made about his drinking and his father couldn't have been easy for him. Knowing more about Jason's background certainly made her understand him better, though she still had her doubts. For instance, he'd said he didn't want to be like his father—but what if he couldn't completely stop himself?

During the meal, they kept their conversation light, catching up on the more everyday aspects of their lives over the past months. Nickie talked about some new clients she was working with and Jason described his projected spring line. He also told her about several new staff members he'd hired at corporate headquarters, and she realized that he was, indeed, gearing down a bit, delegating some of his duties to his subordinates. When he mentioned having hired a new controller, she realized that he probably wasn't going to try to strong-arm her back into working for him. She wondered why this realization caused her a small stab of disappointment.

After lunch, they walked around the corner toward the real-estate office Jason had contacted. Nickie didn't protest when he slipped his hand into hers, and she even smiled at him shyly. On the way, they passed a laughing young couple with a dozing infant in a stroller. The baby—a little girl of about three months—was precious, dressed in a knitted pink cap and matching sweater and booties. Nickie stared at the infant longingly; then she glanced quickly at Jason and saw his jaw tighten as he, too, studied the child. Their gazes locked for a meaningful moment, then his fingers tightly gripped hers as they continued on.

Once they were out of earshot of the happy couple, he said feelingly, "You know, I hope someday we can try for another baby."

Nickie was as startled by his words as she was by the rush of sexual excitement that washed over her. "Don't you think you're putting the cart a little before the horse, Jason?"

"I'm not suggesting we become parents this afternoon," he amended wryly.

Nickie turned away to hide her blush.

Jason tugged on her hand, forcing her to look at him. "Nickie, I thought the purpose of this period was for us to become reacquainted—to examine our thoughts and values and discuss what we both want in the future."

Nickie bit her lip. "Well—I suppose so."

"And I think we need to talk about what went wrong— before."

"I guess you have a point."

"And if you want my opinion, I think a big part of what went wrong is that we lost the baby."

Nickie was suddenly infuriated, stopping and turning to confront him. "That wasn't my fault."

He appeared stunned. "Of course not, darling. I'd never think—" He gripped her by the shoulders and continued urgently, "Nickie, you've missed my point entirely."

"Then what is your point?" she asked, appalled to feel the sting of tears.

"I read an article about this once," he continued. "It said that when a couple, especially a newly married couple, loses a child, it can destroy a marriage. And the only real cure is for the wife to become pregnant again— at once."

Nickie drew a shuddering breath as his words brought forth a host of longings, both physical and emotional. She knew there *had* been a need in her to become pregnant again, ever since she lost the baby, and Jason had just put his finger on a very touchy spot. "Jason, I'll agree that what you're saying makes some sense, but my getting pregnant again would hardly solve all our problems." She shrugged. "But then, I suppose men tend to think issues can be resolved this simplistically."

His hands fell to his sides and he shook his head in a gesture of defeat. "You know, sometimes I think you only went along with this trial reconciliation because of my promise to quit fighting the divorce afterward. You just want to win in the end."

She swallowed a lump that had suddenly risen in her throat and stared at him sadly. "Jason, if things don't work out between us and we do end up divorced, I'd never think of myself as having won."

At that, he smiled at her, brushing a tear from her cheek in a tender gesture that touched her heart. "Thanks for that."

"You're welcome," she whispered.

Jason took her hand and they continued. After a moment, he cleared his throat and asked, "Did you really think I blamed you?"

She glanced at him awkwardly and said, "I felt guilty—responsible somehow."

"You weren't," he stated in a firm, tight voice. "Although I can understand your reactions, since I felt guilty, too—wondering if our problems had somehow precipitated things."

She nodded. "Sometimes I forget that you suffered in this, too."

They basked in a feeling of mutual empathy as they turned into the doorway of the real-estate office. Inside, they were told that the agent Jason had dealt with was still out to lunch, but her boss gave them the key and directions to the shop, which was just two blocks away.

The vacant rental was part of a charming turn-of-the-century brownstone building. The two-story structure had a columned arcade and large display windows on the ground floor; high, arched windows added a quaint touch to the second story. The location of the shop was good, Nickie noted—on a corner with entrances on both sides. Jason struggled for a moment with the stiff lock on the main entrance, then the door swung open and they went inside.

The interior smelled musty from disuse. The layout was cozy, with three levels arranged like ascending stair steps and separated by large archways and stark-white walls. The floors were of stone and fans embellished the high, tin-ceilings. There were elegant supporting columns in the center of each room. Glancing around, Nickie could easily visualize Jason's merchandise beautifully displayed here.

They explored all three levels and the storage/office space at the back. Watching Jason's reactions, Nickie noted a spring in his step and a gleam of excitement in his eye. How he shone when he was planning a new venture, she thought poignantly.

As they stood for a moment on the middle and largest level, Nickie pronounced, "I like it. The architecture is charming and shows some real promise—it's old-fashioned, but just the right backdrop for an eclectic mix of merchandise."

"I agree," Jason said with a smile. "I thought we'd put cosmetics and accessories on the street level—since that would attract the most traffic. The second level could be used for sportswear and dresses, and the third for intimate apparel."

Nickie nodded. "I can see that kind of arrangement working out quite nicely. And the location of the shop is excellent—with the Tremont Hotel just a block away, and all the shops and tourist traffic in the area. Yes, this definitely could be another Stellar Attraction." She fixed a curious smile on him. "But my question remains—why Galveston?"

"Why not?" he replied with a shrug. "Guess I can't resist an untapped market. And I'd like to get this venture going right away, since I'm hoping to time the opening to coincide with Mardi Gras here. I was thinking of a full week of kickoff activities, beginning with Fat Tuesday."

Nickie whistled. "That's in February, Jason. Barely two and a half months away! Don't you think that's biting off a bit more than even you can chew?"

He flashed her his most dazzling smile. "We could do it together."

She rolled her eyes. "Do it together. This from the man who just wanted my opinion, right?"

He closed the distance between them and hugged her. "Babe, I want you, body and soul."

Despite the thrill of his nearness and his sexy words, Nickie fixed him with a challenging frown. "And business acumen?"

"I don't object to a package deal. We were good together—in every way."

She moved out of his arms, not at all reassured by his words. After all, business was what had brought them together in the first place. "So, are you going to take the rental, Jason?"

"Yes."

"You had your mind made up before we even came down here, didn't you?"

"Actually, no. I really did want your opinion."

She sighed. "I suppose you did," she said resignedly.

He glanced at his watch. "Well—shall we go see if the agent is back?"

Nickie was quiet as they left. She felt very confused. On the one hand, Jason showed evidence that he had changed—that he was working less, that he'd quit drinking. Yet on the other hand, here he was, planning to rush into his new venture at a breakneck pace. She couldn't forget that his workaholic tendencies had contributed to the breakup of the marriage before. And she still didn't completely trust his motives. While he'd made no move to try to lure her back into his business full-time, she was very aware that he'd brought her along today, at least in part, as a consultant.

At the real-estate office, they were greeted this time by the listing agent. Sheila Sampson was a beautiful red-head in her early thirties; she was dressed in a snappy woolen suit, wore an expensive perfume and all the right gold accessories. She preened over Jason as if he were a millionaire investor just arrived from Wall Street. "It's so good to meet you at last, Mr. Stellar," she said, warmly shaking his hand. She tossed Nickie a dismissive glance and added, "And this must be the secretary."

"Wife," Jason amended wryly.

Sheila gave Nickie a blank look that informed her in no uncertain terms that the sophisticated realtor consid-

ered her and Jason the original odd couple. But the red-
head soon recovered her composure and conspicuously
ignored Nickie. From the sparkle in her eyes and the way
she even leaned across her desk occasionally to touch
Jason's arm, Nickie suspected that she was trying to sell
more than real estate.

"Look, you don't have to convince us of the merits of
the property," Jason at last interjected, and Nickie noted
with some satisfaction that he had the grace to look embarrassed. "We've already decided to commit to the location."

"Splendid!" Sheila said, clapping her manicured
hands. "This calls for a celebration. May I take you—and
your wife, of course—out for a drink?"

Jason smiled sheepishly. "Actually, just the lease will
do."

Jason and the agent went over the lease in detail, and
she graciously suggested some local contractors and ar-
chitects he could contact regarding renovation of the
shop. By the time they finally got out of the office, Nickie
had had just about all she could stomach of Sheila
Sampson.

"I'm sorry about that, Nickie," Jason said as they
walked back toward his car.

She shrugged. "Women always do find you irresistible."

He grimaced. "Believe me, there are plenty of times
when I wish they wouldn't."

She laughed. "Sorry, but I find that rather hard to believe."

"Do you?" He gestured his frustration. "Think of it
from my perspective. How would you like to be pursued
just for your looks and sex appeal?"

"You think I'm not?" she asked rather defensively.

"Of course, you are," he hastily assured her. "What I'm trying to say is, what if that were the *only* reason you were pursued?"

She mulled that over a minute. "How do you know that's the only reason you're pursued?"

"Well, when a woman comes on that quickly, that strongly—even with my wife present . . . What I'm trying to say is, everyone likes to think he's wanted for himself."

"Yes, I can understand that. I can understand entirely," she said, feeling a rush of sympathy for him. They stared at each other for a moment, then they both broke into a smile.

"So why did you chase after me, Jason?" she asked.

He drew her close and said devilishly, "For your looks and sex appeal."

"Oh, you!"

Even as she tried to shove him away, he kissed her quickly on the nose.

BEFORE LEAVING TOWN, they drove down Seawall Boulevard to catch a glimpse of the Gulf. The waters below looked turbulent; high gray waves, frothed with white, pounded toward the shoreline. Despite the coolness and the agitated waters, a few brave surfers were out.

As they neared their turnoff for Houston, Jason asked, "Nickie, why don't we go to your beach house before we return home. It's too cold for a swim, but we could go for a walk along the beach."

Nickie's breathing quickened at his romantic suggestion. She realized that she desired Jason more than ever, but she wasn't ready for that kind of intimacy or commitment yet, and couldn't risk letting sex cloud the issues—issues like Sheila Sampson and ninety percent of the female population, all of whom found Jason Stellar irresistible!

She cleared her throat noisily. "Jason, I need to get home. I have a whole stack of financial reports to work on this weekend."

"You're sure?" he asked with obvious disappointment.

"I'm sure."

Like the drive down, their drive back to Houston passed mostly in silence. All too soon, they stood at her front door. Nickie stared up at Jason, suddenly hating the fact that their day together was ending. He looked so arresting with the light pouring in from behind him, outlining his tall, lithe body and gleaming in his thick hair. For a moment she almost wished the past—and all her doubts—had ceased to exist.

He seemed to read her thoughts. "Ask me in, Nickie?"

She somehow found the strength to shake her head. "I don't think it would be wise just yet."

He brushed a strand of hair from her brow, and the sensual gleam in his eyes was riveting as he stared back at her. "Did today—help at all?"

He was so serious, so handsome, and so near—Nickie had to struggle to speak. "It was—good. I enjoyed our time together. But it's still a little early to draw any conclusions."

He slipped his arms about her waist and nestled her against his solid strength. "Sure you have to work on all those reports tonight?" he asked huskily.

Clutched so close to his heart, Nickie had to bite her lip to keep from moaning aloud. Jason's scent was filling her senses, his heat was seeping into her, weakening her defenses. She had lied to him, of course; she had only one brief financial report and a budget to complete this weekend. She was planning to spend the rest of her time puttering around the house, addressing a few Christmas cards, watching videos—and doubtless, feeling quite lonely. It would be lovely to have Jason to share the hours with—

He broke into her thoughts. "Well, Nickie?"

She pulled herself together. "I just think it's better if we call it a day."

He tilted her chin with his thumb and forefinger and looked at her intently. "Well, if you won't ask me in, then I at least get a kiss."

Nickie found herself fighting a smile. "Who says you get a kiss?"

He feigned innocence. "That's the way we set up the rules."

"Don't be ridiculous," she retorted primly. "We never agreed to such a rule. I certainly would have remembered."

"Oh, would you?" Watching her blush, he laughed, then his face moved closer to hers. "Hell, maybe it'll be more fun to make up the rules as we go along."

Before Nickie could protest, Jason swooped down to kiss her. His strong arms pulled her upward until her toes left the ground. When his tongue slipped past her teeth, penetrating her mouth with raw hunger, she moaned and kissed him back, pressing her hands eagerly to his face. Even as she ran her fingertips over the warm, slightly rough texture of his skin, Jason slipped a hand inside her sweater, caressing her back. Her nipples tingled in excitement as he crushed her more tightly against him.

When the kiss ended, both were breathing raggedly. "Change your mind, Nickie?" he whispered against her ear.

"Jason, I just can't. Not yet," she replied helplessly. "We've done so well today—don't push it."

He nodded reluctantly. But as he drew back, he traced his finger over her still-wet mouth. "You'll remember this kiss when you have lunch with Jim next week?"

She should have been angered. But he looked so stern, so much like a scolding schoolteacher, that she had to laugh. "Jason, I'm only going to explain things to him. Can't you trust me that much?"

He laughed ruefully. "And this from the girl who doesn't trust *me* at all."

"Don't be ridiculous. Of course, I trust you."

"Really?" he demanded. "How much?"

They stared at each other in tense challenge. At last Nickie sighed and admitted, "I guess not enough."

"Well, at least that's honest," he replied rather grumpily. "I'd say we have our work cut out for us, wouldn't you?"

"I suppose so."

He took the key from her hand and unlocked her door. "Princess, your palace awaits."

She offered him a conciliatory smile. "Thanks for a great day."

He smiled back. "You're most welcome. Call you on Monday."

And then, after ducking down to administer a chaste peck on her cheek, he was gone.

After he left, Nickie lay on her bed, the scent of his cologne still on her hands, the taste of him still on her lips. She hugged a plush yellow duck he'd once won for her at a carnival and watched *An Affair to Remember* on the VCR, wishing he could be there to share the moment with her.

7

DURING THE NEXT FEW weeks, Jason and Nickie continued to see each other frequently. Since they were in the midst of the holiday season, they attended a few Christmas parties given by friends and associates. More often, though, they spent their time alone. They went out to dinner and to concerts, and made several day trips to Galveston to set plans in motion for the new store. These treks weren't just business; each time, they also did something fun, like touring one of the old homes, visiting the railroad museum or riding the trolley.

They talked incessantly—about Jason's new shop, about Nickie's clients, about their lives in general. Although they skirted the more serious issues that had eroded their marriage before—Jason's obsessive behavior, Nickie's lack of trust—the time they spent together was healing. Jason was careful not to pressure Nickie to commit to a permanent reconciliation, but instead made positive comments about their relationship—like, "I've missed doing this with you," or "Weren't we good together today? Didn't we have fun?"

They *did* have fun together, and fun, Nickie had to admit, was hard to resist. Still, she continued to wonder about Jason's motives for wanting her back in his life so badly. For instance, there was the matter of the new store, about which he repeatedly asked her advice. His confidence in her abilities was flattering, of course, but his actions reinforced her fear that he hadn't married her just for herself.

Jason never missed an opportunity to touch her, hug her or wrap his arm about her waist. Every time he said goodbye to her he kissed her, and the kisses grew increasingly intimate. More than once, he left her at her door in a state of seething frustration.

This was particularly true one Saturday in mid-December. Jason and Nickie had gone to Galveston to meet with the architect and several contractors who were renovating the new store; afterward, they stayed late to take a sunset excursion cruise on a paddle wheeler. There were relatively few passengers this crisp early-winter day, and Jason and Nickie had the high promenade deck all to themselves. The setting couldn't have been more romantic or spectacular as they stood at the railing, throwing bread crumbs to the shrieking gulls, feeling the delicious spray of the surf and looking out at the glorious setting. They were both elated by their progress on the Galveston store. The project was running over budget, Jason informed Nickie, but he felt confident that his banker would approve the additional financing needed.

After they'd exhausted the bread crumbs, Jason curled his arms around Nickie's waist, nestling her back against his chest. "Cold?" he asked.

She shook her head and gazed happily at the dancing gray waves. "I'm enjoying myself far too much to be cold."

"Thanks for your help today, Nickie," he said sincerely.

"My pleasure."

"You know, I think you were right about the carpet color, and the decorator was wrong."

Nickie laughed wryly as she recalled their meeting with the middle-aged, rather pretentious interior decorator. "Phyllis didn't appreciate having that pointed out."

"You were tactful enough about it. Still, the color she wanted was too bold. I also love your idea of redoing the pillars in faux marble."

"It seems popular these days."

He nodded. "We make a good team, Nickie."

His words were sobering, reminding her that he might have an ulterior motive in wanting them back together. But she thrust her doubts aside, refusing to let anything spoil this beautiful moment. Jason's nearness felt so warm, so right.

"I've never seen a more beautiful sunset," she murmured.

He leaned over to press his cool lips against her cheek. "You know, we could stay over and see the sunrise, too, darling. Just say the word."

It was an electrifying moment for Nickie. Her heart pounded in her chest, and she turned in Jason's arms to look at him. The sensual intensity reflected in his beautiful blue eyes left her knees weak. She realized that making love with Jason would be the perfect culmination of a wonderful day—and it could also be disastrous to make a physical commitment when she still wasn't ready emotionally.

She wrinkled her nose at him. "For now, let's just savor the sunset, okay?"

"Okay," he agreed reluctantly.

But Jason pulled her even closer as the wind gusted, her back against him. He slipped his hands under her heavy sweater, cupping her breasts through her bra.

"Jason!" she gasped.

"We're all alone, my dear," he said, leaning over to press his lips against her throat. "And may I remind you that we're married?"

As the pulse in her throat jumped wildly beneath the pressure of his lips, Nickie was about to say that she didn't have to be reminded that they were married—not at all. But before she could speak, he turned her face to him, capturing her mouth. His lips tasted deliciously cool and slightly salty; his tongue was hot as it pressed deep into her mouth, swirling sensuously. His fingers dug into her aching, aroused breasts and his hips moved provocatively against her. Nickie shuddered in ecstasy, feeling deliciously dizzy and aroused.

When the kiss ended, Jason pressed his cheek against hers and she leaned into his strength to keep her balance, taking in short, sharp breaths.

"Stay with me tonight, Nickie?" he whispered.

Nickie's mouth trembled as her eyes met his apologetically. "Jason, it's still too soon."

With a deep sigh, he released her. He strolled off a few feet and stood staring at the horizon. Watching him, she sighed, too. She could gauge his frustration level from the way his fists were shoved into his pockets; his wind-tousled hair was an unspeakably sexy crown for his scowling visage.

Nickie grasped the railing to hold on to her equilibrium.

THE FOLLOWING WEEK, Nickie took pains to avoid being alone with Jason, to restrict their dates to more public places. Jason was coming on stronger sexually now, and she was running scared.

To make things worse, she feared she was falling in love again—feared that Jason was insinuating himself so deeply into her heart that she could never break free of his spell. The memory of her and Jason kissing on the steamboat haunted her; sometimes at night, she would awaken trembling with unfulfilled desire and she could again feel the rhythm of the boat and the delicious pressure of his lips on hers. The chemistry between them had always been potent, and she found that time had only intensified that fierce, inexorable longing.

Her reactions to Jason now were frighteningly similar to those she'd experienced during the captivating days when she'd first met him. She had intended to go into this second courtship with her eyes wide open; now she feared that love was again putting the blinders on.

Despite her softening attitude toward Jason, Nickie still couldn't shake her doubts that the same problems might resurface and spoil their relationship a second time. What if Jason distanced himself from her and became obsessed with his work again? What if he were just using her to get the new store off the ground? She still feared that at some point he would lose interest in her in favor of someone much more glamorous—someone more like himself.

After all, that's what her father had done to her mother—abandoning her later in life for a younger, more sophisticated woman. Nickie had once read an article about the "trophy" wives some men pursued in their later years. Would Jason, too, be one of those men who couldn't face losing the robust virility of his youth, a man who would eventually need a young glamour doll to feed his ego?

ON THURSDAY MORNING, Nickie sat in her office trying to tie up some loose ends so she could get off to a business meeting. Jason had offered to cook dinner for them tonight, but she hadn't trusted herself to spend the evening alone with him. Since her business meeting was in his building, she had offered instead to meet him at the cafeteria for lunch. She had made her suggestion in an attempt to keep a safe distance between them, and she suspected that he saw straight through her ploy. Indeed, he hadn't been very enthusiastic about her idea and would have preferred to take her out for a longer meal at an intimate restaurant nearby. But when Nickie had insisted that her schedule was tight today, he'd grudgingly agreed to her plan.

Nickie was ready to leave when the phone rang.

"Hi, sis, are you okay?" the caller asked.

Nickie at once recognized the voice of her older sister, Meredith. She felt a stab of guilt that she hadn't called her pregnant sister in several weeks. "Oh, hi, Mere. Gee, I've been meaning to call you. How's my future niece or nephew doing?"

"Just great—though the little beggar is really wearing me out these days."

"You're due pretty soon now, aren't you?"

"December 31. Richard is already moaning and groaning because he's sure I'll deliver a day late and we won't get an extra tax deduction this year."

Nickie laughed. Meredith was married to a tax attorney. "As a CPA, I can sympathize."

"You bean counters," Meredith teased. More seriously, she continued, "Hey, Nick, you sounded rather harried when you answered just now. Am I keeping you from something?"

She glanced at her watch. "Actually, I need to get off for a meeting with a client. But I can talk for a few minutes first."

"What about you and Jason?" Meredith went on. "We haven't spoken for weeks, and the last I heard from you, you were really feeling frustrated about the divorce."

Nickie paused in uncertainty. She knew that a major reason she hadn't called her sister recently was that Meredith had always insisted that Nickie's wanting a divorce from Jason was a big mistake. And as much as Nickie loved her sister, she didn't need anyone else undermining her convictions right now; Jason was already doing a first-rate job at that!

"Well, Nickie?" Meredith prodded.

Cautiously Nickie admitted, "Actually, Jason and I have decided to put the divorce on hold for the moment."

"You have?"

Nickie heard the excitement in her sister's voice. "Don't jump to any conclusions, Mere. It's just that Jason out-and-out refused to quit fighting the divorce unless I first agreed to a trial reconciliation."

"Are you sleeping with him, Nickie?"

"Meredith!" Nickie could feel her face flaming.

"I think you'd be a fool not to. That man is a living doll. If not for Richard, hon, I'd be chasing right after him myself."

Nickie rolled her eyes. "And this from a woman almost nine months pregnant. Meredith, you're impossible."

Meredith's effervescent laughter proved that she was far from contrite. "I hope you're not going along with Jason just so you'll get your divorce in the end. I know he really hurt you before, and I can understand that. But please give him another chance—people *do* change."

"Now you're sounding like Jason," Nickie accused. "Don't tell me he nudged you into this little phone call?"

"Don't be ridiculous. I haven't even seen Jason since the two of you broke up."

Nickie sighed. "Sorry, I didn't mean to sound so defensive. For the record, I am trying to give Jason a chance."

"Great."

"And I haven't asked you why you called in the first place."

"Oh, right. Actually, it's about Christmas."

"Christmas?"

"Mom and Steve were wondering if you're planning to spend it with the family."

Nickie smiled poignantly. For the past few Christmases, her mother and stepdad had hosted a family gathering for Vivian's three grown children and their families. Nickie had attended last year—with Jason. The thought of attending alone this year was rather dispiriting.

"Yes, of course I'll come," she said at last.

"You can bring Jason," Meredith suggested.

Nickie stifled a groan. "Look, Mere, it's too soon to say whether Jason and I are going to make it in the long run."

"You mean you'd shut him out just for the sake of appearances?" her sister asked indignantly.

"There's a lot more to it than that," Nickie countered.

"Nickie, quit being so cautious and think of this from Jason's perspective for a change. Isn't his father dead and his mother living back East somewhere?"

Nickie winced. "Yes. Jason almost never hears from her."

"And you're going to desert him on Christmas?"

"Mere, I'll think about it, okay?"

"Okay. And I'll tell Mom and Steve that you're coming for sure on Christmas."

"Thanks. Let's get together for lunch soon. Perhaps on Saturday?"

"It's a date, kid."

Nickie hung up the phone feeling perturbed. She'd always felt a little in awe of her glamorous older sister. Meredith had it all—looks, brains, plus a great personality. Meredith had been on the fast track to success as a local news anchorwoman when she'd met and married wealthy tax attorney Richard Crawford. Now, a year later, the two were about to have their first child, and Nickie had to admit that she'd stayed away from her sister in part because Meredith's pregnancy was a painful reminder of her own loss. She knew she was being unfair there, and that she must do better. Despite the fact that the sisters had never been exceptionally close, Meredith had always been a loyal, supportive sister. Now, Nickie vowed she wouldn't let her sister down at this critical time in her life.

NICKIE'S MEETING WITH engineer George Wilson went extremely well; in fact, she landed her biggest account ever at Wilson Engineering that morning. George was impressed by her plan to streamline his accounting procedures, and he even offered her a job on the spot. Although pleased, Nickie declined. George was midthirtyish, unmarried, balding but affable—the type of man she might have pursued if Jason hadn't come along. She couldn't help but feel flattered that George seemed disappointed not just on a professional level but on a personal level, too.

Elated, she left his office to meet Jason for lunch. She spotted her husband at once in the lounge area outside the cafeteria. Dressed in an impeccable gray pin-stripe suit, a white shirt and a maroon tie, he stood frowning at his watch—and looking totally adorable, she decided. In fact, he looked so debonair, she was glad that she'd worn her new royal blue wool suit and a coordinating print-silk blouse.

As she approached, he glanced up and spotted her. Grinning, he strode quickly to her side and kissed her on the cheek. "Hi, hon— Wow you look great."

"So do you," she replied with a smile.

They got their trays and moved toward the salad bar. "How did your meeting go?" he asked.

"Fantastic," she replied brightly. "In fact, landing a prestigious firm like Wilson Engineering will be a big feather in my cap at work."

He smiled. "Congratulations, then."

"Thanks."

Yet Nickie frowned to herself as she spooned marinated vegetables onto her plate. She had noted a degree of reserve in Jason's response, and she suspected that he wasn't completely thrilled by her success this morning. Perhaps he feared that her expanding client base might take more of her time—or, she thought more unkindly, interfere with their work together on the new store.

She flashed him a quick smile. "It's great that my meeting was here in your building, so we could meet like this."

That remark won her a glower. "I still would have preferred to take you out."

"I'm really rushed today, and this is perfect," Nickie insisted.

"It's not so perfect when you eat here practically everyday," he continued with the same ill-humor. "And the atmosphere is anything but intimate."

"Come on, Jason—be a sport," she teased.

They settled in at a small table near a glass wall and began their lunch with the usual small talk. Both remarked on the dreary landscape outside and the chilly, wet weather. Noting the Christmas decorations displayed about the room, Nickie mused that they'd have to decide very soon whether they'd spend the holiday together.

Only minutes after they'd sat down, Nickie noticed George Wilson leaving the serving line and crossing the dining room. As she might have predicted, he stopped by their table.

"Hi, Nickie, it's good to see you again so soon," he said, smiling.

"Hi, George," she replied pleasantly. "I'd like you to meet my—er—husband, Jason Stellar. Jason, this is George Wilson."

The two men shook hands. "Pleased to meet you," Jason said in a clipped voice that sounded anything but pleased.

"So, you're the lucky Mr. Stellar," George replied, seemingly oblivious to Jason's chilly reception. "You know, I tried to woo your wife away this morning."

Nickie felt herself blushing as Jason asked softly, ominously, "Did you?"

George grinned. "Offered her a job, but she turned me down flat. Too bad, since I feel she'd be a real asset to our firm. But I plan to keep trying—that is, if you have no objection, Mr. Stellar."

"Be my guest," Jason said affably.

Nickie glanced at George's full tray. "Won't you join us?"

He shook his head. "Thanks, but I'm meeting some colleagues. Well, enjoy your lunch, you two," he added, heading off again.

A tense silence descended after George left. Nickie nibbled at her shepherd's pie and avoided Jason's eyes; but she could feel the heat of his gaze on her.

"So your meeting went very well," Jason said sarcastically. "A job offer, Nickie?"

Nickie dropped her fork and looked him in the eye. "And that is exactly the reason I didn't tell you about it."

"Reason? What reason? Do I look upset?"

"Yes."

"You'd work for him, but you wouldn't work for me," he accused.

She gestured in exasperation. "Jason, I turned him down. And besides, you haven't even asked me to work for you again."

He leaned toward her, taking her hand. "And if I did?" he asked in a low, intimate tone.

The timbre of his voice and the touch of his fingers on hers battered her resolve. She sighed. "You know I don't think it's wise that I get too heavily involved in your business. Not at this point."

He harrumphed. "I think George is interested in a lot more than business."

She flashed her eyes up to his. "He's a friendly man. Jason, you can't expect me never to be around other men. Look at what you do, for heaven's sake."

"Did you have to ask him to join us?" he asked irritably.

"What else was I supposed to do? He's a very important client."

"More important than your husband, I presume?"

She rolled her eyes. "Jason, for heaven's sake!"

He was unable to continue the argument, as one of his employees stopped by the table to say hello. The young man, a new employee with Jason's corporation, was obviously trying to ingratiate himself with his boss; he left only after Jason dropped several broad hints.

"This place is entirely too friendly," Jason complained when at last they were alone again. "We should have boxed up our lunches and taken them back to my office."

"Come on, Jason, it's not that bad." Before he could protest further, she said, "So, tell me—have there been any more developments regarding the new store?"

He laughed dryly. "Actually, Phyllis called yesterday and informed me almost gleefully that the carpet color you selected has been discontinued by the factory."

"Oh, no!"

They laughed over this and other small complications that had arisen regarding the new store. Nickie was feeling relieved that she'd evidently cheered Jason out of his ill-humor when he abruptly asked, "You finished with your lunch?"

"Well, yes."

"Then let's go."

Nickie struggled to hide her disappointment, since she'd been enjoying her brief time with him. "Already?"

He shot her a smoldering look. "I'd prefer to spend the rest of your meager lunch-hour visiting in my office."

Nickie started to protest, then thought better of it as she studied his darkly determined expression. "Okay, then."

As they started off with their trays, she added, "You're in a strange mood today."

"Is it a crime to want to be alone with my wife?" He took her hand as they left the cafeteria and went to his office, to the familiar glass double doors on which Stellar Attractions was inscribed in understated gold lettering.

As they swept inside the large, elegant front office, the receptionist waved to them as she worked the switchboard. They continued on, pausing at the secretary's desk outside Jason's office. A lovely young blonde manned the desk. "Hi, Mr. Stellar," she said brightly. Her gaze fixed confusedly on Nickie.

Jason quickly filled the gap. "Nickie, I'd like you to meet my new secretary, Stephanie Burns. Stephanie, this is my wife, Nickie Stellar."

"Hi, Stephanie," Nickie said with a smile, extending her hand.

"Your wife?" Stephanie repeated, staring blankly at Jason. "I thought you were getting a—I mean, you hadn't mentioned..." Recovering her composure, she quickly shook the hand Nickie offered and said, "I'm so pleased to meet you, Mrs. Stellar."

"Please, call me Nickie," Nickie murmured.

"Nickie's such a prize, I like to keep her under wraps," Jason added, winking at his secretary.

Stephanie blushed. "Why, of course." She hesitated, then added to Jason, "Well, did you and—er—your wife have a good lunch?"

"Oh, the best," Jason said sarcastically. "Half the building stopped by our table. You really should have joined us, too."

"Well—sure," Stephanie stammered, blushing again, while Nickie tossed her husband a perplexed glance.

Undaunted, Jason took Nickie's hand. "Stephanie, my wife and I need to talk for a few minutes. Please hold all my calls?"

"Certainly, Mr. Stellar."

As Jason led Nickie off, she glanced over her shoulder, catching Stephanie's lost, poignant expression as she stared after Jason.

Inside his office, he shut the door, took off his coat and hung it on the hook. "Have a seat, Nickie."

Nickie glanced briefly at the familiar furnishings—the massive mahogany desk, the tufted leather chairs and settee, the expensive contemporary paintings and handsome brass accessories. Foregoing Jason's offer of a chair, she wandered over to the stark floor-to-ceiling windows that lined one wall. She stared grimly at the grayness outside and took a moment to gather her thoughts. She hadn't appreciated Jason's flirtatious comment to Stephanie in the outer office—but then, he'd clearly made his remark to retaliate for her having invited George to join them at lunch.

Jason came over to join her now, resting a hand on her shoulder. For a moment, both of them stared out at the skyscrapers shrouded in gray mist.

She turned to look up at him. "I see you've replaced the blonde in the outer office."

He laughed in surprise. "Oh, you mean Stephanie?"

"Yes. What happened to Anne?"

"She had a baby. We wanted her back after her maternity leave, but she decided to stay home and raise her child."

Nickie's heartstrings tugged at the thought. "Can't say I blame her."

"Neither can I."

They fell silent again. Nickie cleared her throat. "Stephanie seems an excellent replacement—in fact, she looks enough like Anne to be her twin."

Jason's hand tightened on her shoulder. "Are you implying that I select my secretaries by looks alone?"

Nickie turned to face him. "Do you?"

He frowned. "My secretary has to meet and greet a lot of important people."

"And appearances are very important to you, aren't they, Jason?"

He shook his head incredulously. "I can't believe you're making an issue out of this."

"I'm not making an issue out of it," she said defensively. "It's just an observation."

"Is it?" He crossed his arms over his chest and clenched his jaw. "For your information, Stellar Attractions hires people of all physical types and age groups, with varying levels of experience—"

"I'm aware of that, but—"

"And furthermore, Stephanie Burns came to us with excellent training and references. In fact, it was Anne who did the initial interviewing and recommended Stephanie as a temporary replacement."

"How nice for you."

His eyes glittered with annoyance and his arms fell to his sides. "What is this, Nickie? You don't usually give me the third degree regarding my employees."

"She's in love with you."

"Who?"

"Stephanie."

He looked taken aback. "You're kidding."

"Not at all. It's written all over her face. She looked devastated when you showed up with me. Don't tell me you didn't notice?"

He raked a hand through his hair. "Actually, I didn't. Guess my mind is somewhere else." He stared pointedly at her.

"Why didn't you tell her that we've put the divorce on hold?"

"Because my personal life is—was—none of her business," he answered with sudden anger. "Do you think I discuss our relationship with just anyone?"

She shrugged. "It still seems odd that you didn't mention the reconciliation to her." Resentfully she added, "And I can't believe you told her she should have joined us for lunch."

"Aha!" he exclaimed. "So, that's why you're in such a snit! It's perfectly fine for you to ask George Wilson to join us, but if I make a friendly overture toward my secretary, all of a sudden I'm a shameless philanderer."

Nickie was exasperated. "Jason, there's a difference. I was just being congenial toward a client, while you were encouraging a woman who is obviously in love with you."

"It's not different, and you know it," he retorted. "Furthermore, if you think there was nothing amorous in George Wilson's attitude toward you, then, honey, I'm very concerned about your naïveté."

Nickie's cheeks flamed at Jason's bald words. She knew he'd used the entire incident to make a point—but he'd also succeeded. "Well, you don't have to act condescending about it," she said irritably. "You're just trying to cloud the issue—"

"No," he cut in, "you're trying to impose some ridiculous double standard here. Nickie, do you actually believe that just because a woman finds me attractive, I automatically drag her off to my cave like some Neanderthal?"

Despite herself, she fought a smile. "It would seem a natural enough temptation for a man like you."

He threw up his hands and paced to the door, where he surprised her by throwing the latch.

"Jason?" she asked, confused.

He strode over to his desk and sat down, loosening his tie. "Come over here," he said.

She eyed him cautiously, but found his implacable features gave no real hint of his feelings. She walked over to his desk, tilting her chin defiantly as she met his gaze.

He took her hand and stared up at her intently. "It's not so simple, Nickie. You're not going to get out of this by picking a fight with me."

Intrigued, she asked, "Get out of what?"

Abruptly he caught her around the waist, pulling her down onto his lap. "Being alone with me."

"Jason!" Caught off guard, she protested, "Stephanie—"

"The door is locked and Stephanie's holding my calls," he said with a smug smile.

"Still, you shouldn't—"

"Hush," he said, and kissed her.

Nickie's further protests were smothered by Jason's bold, thorough lips. Even as his mouth drank hungrily of hers, his impatient hands unbuttoned her jacket and tugged it off. He caressed her back and arms through the thin silk of her blouse and didn't stop kissing her until she was soft and pliant in his arms.

"Still determined to fight me?" he asked at last.

Nickie caught her breath, rubbed a finger across her throbbing lips and stared at him with wide, languorous eyes. "Women always fall in love with you," she said morosely.

"So that's the real issue," he replied soberly.

She swallowed hard. "Yes."

He traced his fingertips over the curve of her jaw. "And what about you, Nickie Stellar?"

She sighed heavily. "I guess I'm no more immune to your charms than any other woman."

"Oh, Nickie." He caught her close and nuzzled his lips against her cheek. "Do you really think I'd be interested in Stephanie?"

She shivered delightedly and wrapped her arms around his neck. His nearness had such a way of turning her to mush! "Oh, I don't know," she muttered. "'Stephanie Stellar.' It has a nice ring to it."

"I don't want a Stephanie Stellar. I want you," he growled, kissing her again.

Nickie sighed and surrendered to his masterful kiss. It did feel wonderful and rather wicked, sitting here with him, surrounded by his strength and absorbing his scent, tasting the magic of his lips on hers and listening to the rough sound of his breathing.

"What are you trying to do?" she murmured.

He chuckled, but his eyes had a dangerous intensity. "Seduce you," he whispered back.

"Here? In this chair?" she asked with a laugh.

"Nickie, it's time," he said passionately, undoing the tie on her blouse. He removed her glasses and stared into her eyes. "Do you have any idea how crazy you've been driving me? All the time we've spent together these last weeks, kissing, holding hands.... Not to mention the memories of when we didn't have to stop like that." He uttered a low, frustrated moan. "Honey, you've been handing out hors d'oeuvres to a man accustomed to a seven-course meal."

Nickie had to smile there. Hadn't she felt these same frustrations herself?

"Look, it's Thursday," he continued in a sexy, persuasive tone. "Let me call my travel agent to book us on a flight. Let's go somewhere isolated and make love all weekend."

As much as his words thrilled her, making sanity recede, Nickie managed a feeble protest. "No, Jason, it's still too soon." But her words died as Jason kissed her breast. He was sucking provocatively on her nipple through her bra, and he couldn't have aroused her more if he'd stripped her naked. "Oh, Jason," she moaned.

"It's okay—I don't mind making love to you right here," he said huskily. "As for this chair, I think it's just perfect." He looked up at her flushed, breathless face. "You're perfect—so small we both fit in this wonderful chair. Look—I can place your knees around me just so, and take you right here in my lap."

By now, Nickie was going crazy, reeling with delight as Jason's hands raised her skirt and settled firmly on her bottom. Even as his fingers tugged on her panty hose, she could feel his hard arousal pressing against the front of her, and she throbbed and ached in response.

Jason nibbled at her shoulder. "A Stephanie Stellar would never fit in a position like this—or in my life. And a Stephanie Stellar would never be so much fun to undo."

"I'm fun to undo?"

"You're delightful to undo. No one is right for me but you, Nickie. No one."

Nickie could only moan and cling to him.

"Touch me, Nickie," he pleaded, when the phone rang.

They both jumped, and Jason uttered a furious expletive as he grabbed the line. "What is it?" he barked. Nickie tried to spring out of his lap, but he held her tightly. "Okay, put him on." Moving the receiver away from his face, he murmured to her, "Hang on a moment, hon. Please."

Nickie remained captive, straddling Jason, while he had a brief conversation with his banker. It was just enough time for her to realize how ridiculous she must look and what a terrible mistake she'd almost made. After all, the evidence of what she was up against was sitting in Jason's outer office. She could never compete with all the "Stephanie Stellar" types who wanted him—and even if Jason claimed to be oblivious to their charms, sooner or later, one of them was bound to snag him. And Jason's flirtatious comment to Stephanie still bothered her—as did the fact that he hadn't told his secretary about their reconciliation.

"Hey, that's great," Jason was saying, in a polite, if strained voice. "I'm glad the additional financing has been approved." As Nickie once again tried to bolt, his arm clenched about her middle and he glowered at her. "Talk to you soon, Sam."

He hung up the phone. "Sorry, Nickie. But as I'm sure you heard, that was my banker—and the additional financing for the new store has been lined up. I can't blame Stephanie for putting the call through—she knew how important it was to me." He grinned devilishly and ran his hand over her smooth stomach, raising her slip. "Now, where were we?"

"On the brink of seduction," Nickie managed wryly, trying to tug her slip out of his strong fingers. "Please, Jason, let me up. I've got to go."

"Nickie, we can go somewhere more private."

She shook her head. "It's just not right. Not yet."

"Damn it, Nickie, there's nothing going on between Stephanie and me."

"I didn't say there was."

He sighed and released her, watching her stand and right her clothing. "Go away with me this weekend?"

"Jason, please stop crowding me." Her trembling fingers refused to tie the bow on her blouse, and she bit her lip in consternation.

He stood and began tying her bow. "I don't mean to crowd you, honey. It's just that— Damn, if only the blasted phone hadn't rung."

She tossed a strand of hair from her eyes. "Your business is very important to you. It always has been."

Finished with the bow, he frowned. "I don't like the way you said that, or the way we're parting on this. There's a lot more we need to discuss."

"Okay, but can we make it later? I'll be late for my two o'clock—"

"If you won't go away with me this weekend, then at least promise to spend Christmas with me," he cut in obdurately. "It's less than ten days away now."

She shook her head miserably. "I can't, Jason."

"Then give me something, Nickie," he pleaded.

Near the breaking point, she blurted, "Okay. How about Christmas Eve? Can we compromise on that?"

He lit up like a young kid. "I get the whole day!"

She nodded tremulously. "You've got a deal."

Nickie grabbed her purse and left Jason's office while she could still hang on to her resolution. What daunted her the most was the fact that a big part of her sorely wished that Jason's phone had never rung.

8

"CONTACT LENSES? Meredith, you've got to be kidding!"

Nickie and her sister Meredith were seated in the food court of Memorial City Mall, having a light lunch before they finished their Saturday shopping. The mall was noisy and bright today, with Christmas carols spilling from overhead speakers as shoppers milled about.

Meredith had just stunned Nickie by announcing that she wanted to buy her contact lenses for Christmas. Now, as Nickie protested, she studied her older sister. Even in her ninth month of pregnancy, Meredith was a striking beauty with her shoulder-length ash-blond hair, large blue eyes and oval face. Today she was dressed in a stylish navy wool dress.

Imminent motherhood hadn't caused Meredith to lose any of her effervescence, Nickie noted. Meredith finished swallowing a bite of salad and winked at her sister conspiratorially. "I've already made an appointment with the ophthalmologist for next week during your lunch hour, and I insist that you go. If you don't stall around on this, you can have the lenses in time for your Christmas Eve date with Jason."

"Mere, I tried contact lenses when I was a teenager and they drove me crazy."

"There have been enormous improvements in the lenses since then," Meredith argued. "I want you to try soft lenses, like what I wear. If they drive you crazy, too, so be it. But you *are* going to try the lenses again. You've been hiding those lovely brown eyes far too long. You've never done enough to accentuate what you have."

Nickie rolled her supposedly "lovely" brown orbs. "All right, if you insist, I'll go see the ophthalmologist. But you know darned well that there's nothing pretty about me. You're the gorgeous one in the family, taking after Dad. As for Mack, Jr., and me—we're both unspectacular in the looks department, like Mom."

Meredith slanted her younger sister a reproachful look. "Nickie, why do you keep insisting you're not attractive? You're really downright cute. How could you have hooked Jason Stellar if you weren't?"

Nickie frowned as she stirred her iced tea. "I really don't know how I hooked Jason Stellar."

"Have you ever thought that things are more difficult for people like Jason and me?" Meredith went on. "Perhaps we are more attractive than some—but that has to make us wonder if we're wanted for our looks alone."

"Jason's pretty much said the same thing," Nickie admitted.

"And it's true. If you're not a raving beauty, Nick, then that should only convince you that Jason wants you for yourself."

Yet Nickie's expression remained troubled. "I think Jason married me because he's a traditionalist in some ways."

"What do you mean?"

Nickie hesitated, then confessed, "I was a virgin when I met him, and I think there's a part of him that liked the old-fashioned idea of marrying a girl who came to him 'innocent.' At any rate, he's always gone wild at the thought of me being with other men—even though he's around other women constantly."

"And you think he's jealous only because he was your first?"

"I'm not sure." Sighing, Nickie leaned back in her chair. "Frankly, Meredith, I'm confused about everything right now—but especially about sex."

Meredith smirked. "Are you sleeping with him yet?"

Nickie flung a hand wide in exasperation. "Meredith, what is it with you, always giving me the third degree about this? Not that I should be surprised—you always were the devilish one in the family."

"And you always were altogether too sober and strait-laced about everything." Meredith leaned forward and wrinkled her nose mischievously. "So, are you sleeping with him?"

"No!" Squirming in her chair, Nickie amended, "At least, not at the moment." Watching Meredith's eyes widen, she cleared her throat and hastily forged on: "You see, I want to get some important issues resolved first. Still, it's becoming more of a cat-and-mouse game every time Jason and I are together."

Meredith laughed, flashing delightful dimples. "Men are so direct."

"And how," Nickie seconded. Biting her lip, she confided, "In fact, sometimes I'm afraid that a major reason Jason wants me back is because—well, our love life was good."

"Oh, I don't think that's the only reason, Nickie," Meredith said seriously. "Sure, sex is important to men, but a good physical relationship alone won't make a marriage work. It's just that men see sex differently from us. They're really very insecure, and it drives them crazy when we shut them out. The basic dilemma seems to be pretty much what you said—we women want all the issues settled up front, while men tend to think everything can be resolved in bed. With a guy, it's always, 'Let's go to bed, hon, and discuss it later.'"

Nickie giggled. "Is Richard like that?"

"Oh, yes, although he's pretty much my captive audience these days." The sisters convulsed into laughter, then Meredith winked at Nickie. "So, what are you waiting for, kid?"

"Oh, I don't know...." Nickie bit her lip. "I just want to be sure—I mean, I want to know that I'm wanted for myself."

Meredith shook her head slowly. "You really can't trust him, can you Nickie?"

Nickie met her sister's gaze and said miserably, "Mere, you know what happened nine months ago, at the hospital, when I smelled Tracy's perfume and—"

"So some model tried to seduce him, and you freaked out," Meredith summed up with a wave of a slim hand. "It was entirely to be expected under the circumstances." Leaning forward, Meredith touched Nickie's arm and said, "Look, honey, just because a guy's drop-dead gorgeous doesn't mean he's a Casanova."

"You mean, a guy like our father?" Nickie asked bitterly.

"Aha! There we have it." Meredith wagged a finger at Nickie. "Before you met Jason, the only real male role model in your life was a man about as trustworthy as a tomcat turned loose in a feline grooming parlor. Think about that, kiddo."

Nickie laughed ruefully. "Actually, I have."

"You know it's not fair to blame Jason just because of Dad."

"Oh, Meredith." Nickie shook her head as she remembered Jason's comment to Stephanie a few days ago.

"I just wish things were that simple. Have you heard from Dad lately?"

Meredith fingered her paper cup and glanced at Nickie sheepishly. "Nick, I've been meaning to tell you. Mom's planning a big get-together in the spring, for whenever we have the baby christened. And . . . she's planning to invite Dad and his wife from California."

"You're kidding!"

Meredith shook her head.

"After all the hell he put Mom through, walking out on her with that—bimbo?" Nickie asked indignantly.

"Nick, Sandra isn't a bimbo."

Nickie sighed. "Okay, you're right. That was a cheap shot on my part. Still, she broke up Mom and Dad's marriage—"

"Hon, we don't know what Dad told Sandra about his marital status at the time, or what was really going on between him and Mom," Meredith cut in intently. "And while I'm certainly not defending the man, he did live up to his obligation to us kids, sending us all through school." Throwing Nickie a compassionate glance, she added, "I know you're still bitter, but don't you think maybe it's time to bury the hatchet?"

Nickie lifted her chin defensively. "Speak for yourself. Anyway, I'm stunned that Mom would even consider asking him out for the christening."

"Life is short. Maybe Mom's tired of all this hostility. And the man does have a right to see his grandchild."

Nickie shrugged. "I suppose you have a point." She forced a brighter tone. "Speaking of which, since you're insisting on fitting me up with contact lenses, I am now going to buy my future niece or nephew the most lavish, frivolous gift I can find. And I think we need to do it quickly, since we don't want to overtax an expectant mother."

"I do tire more easily these days," Meredith admitted.

"Then let's get going before the mall bursts with shoppers."

TRUE TO HER PROMISE to Meredith, Nickie went to the eye doctor early the following week and was fitted with contact lenses. She had to admit that Meredith was right—the soft lenses were much more comfortable than the hard variety she'd tried as a teenager. Within days, she had completely adjusted to the new lenses. What was harder was looking into the mirror and seeing a new person. The bookish quality of her appearance was missing now. She realized Meredith was right—she did look almost cute. And the fact that she caught more stares than usual from the opposite sex reinforced the new vision of herself.

She didn't see Jason at all—not until their date on Christmas Eve. Nickie dressed with care that morning, choosing white wool slacks and a hot-pink cashmere sweater. When Jason arrived at nine-thirty, he eyed her with delight. "Hey, you look good enough to hang on my Christmas tree. But aren't you forgetting your glasses?"

Nickie shook her head as she, in turn, admired him in his leather jacket and dark slacks. She realized how much she had missed him this week, how thrilled she was to see him. "Meredith insisted on giving me contact lenses for Christmas."

"And you're wearing them now?"

"Yes." Tentatively she asked, "What do you think?"

He grinned, then chucked her under the chin playfully. "I'm not sure I approve. You look too cute."

"'Cute.' That's what Meredith called me."

"And you are." He forced a menacing scowl. "In fact, I'm not sure I want to turn you loose in the malls looking so fetching."

Laughing, she turned to get her coat from its hook near the door. "Maybe that's why you married me."

"What do you mean, why I married you?"

Turning with her coat in hand, she mumbled, "Maybe you're just a basic possessive type, and you'd prefer to have a wife who doesn't attract too much male traffic."

He helped her don her jacket and glanced at her reprovingly. "It couldn't be because I wanted little old you, right?"

"Well, maybe you *think* you did, but—"

"Nickie," he interrupted impatiently, grasping her by the shoulders, "when are you going to stop this analysis crap and let me tell you what my true feelings are?"

She chewed her bottom lip. "Now I've made you mad. Look, if we want to finish our last-minute Christmas shopping, we'd better go before the malls get completely crazy, right?"

"Right."

She grabbed her purse and they hurried out the door into the clear, chilly day. Yet once they were in his car driving away, Nickie murmured, "My dad was like that."

"Like what?"

"He always ran around on Mom. And I really think he married someone plain like her because he didn't want the competition."

"I'm sorry, Nickie," Jason said sincerely.

"Meredith told me that Mom is planning to invite Dad and his wife out for the baby's christening next year," Nickie went on.

"And you find that threatening?" he asked gently.

"Yes," she admitted. "My relationship with him has been strained ever since he walked out on the family."

Jason was quiet, frowning thoughtfully as they moved through the heavy traffic. "You know, I never walked out on you, Nickie," he said at last. "You did all the walking."

She stared at him through sudden tears. "I know."

Yet Jason was frowning to himself as he turned his car into the parking lot of the Galleria. There was so much pain in Nickie, and sometimes, he felt so helpless. Obviously, her father had really hurt her in the past, just as he had hurt her during their marriage. He deeply regretted his actions then. Yet he had also changed. Really changed. *When* would she believe that?

9

THE GALLERIA WASN'T too crowded when Jason and Nickie arrived at ten. Walking down the second-level catwalk, they held hands and admired the endless streamers of tiny white lights cascading from the high domed ceiling above them, while below, ice skaters twirled on the center rink. Every store was festooned with garlands and Christmas trees, and a different carol spilled from each doorway they passed.

They stopped first at Jason's crowded store. While Jason spoke with his manager, Claude White, Nickie chuckled over the chrome mannequins cleverly decked out in "Santa" rompers, black tights and dark glasses. Glancing at the two men deeply immersed in conversation, she smiled to herself. She realized that Jason's reserving all of Christmas Eve for her had to have been a sacrifice, as busy as he was right now. Yet, he'd done so eagerly—a gesture that endeared him to her.

Once he returned to her side, they browsed at a table of sweaters. Nickie helped Jason select a gray cardigan for his cleaning lady. The salesgirl was all smiles and blushes as she proudly wrapped the package for "Mr. Stellar *himself*," going to great lengths to make her gift-wrapping job a real tour de force. A couple of other clerks ventured over to watch, while he chatted politely with the women and shifted uncomfortably from foot to foot. Indeed, he created such a stir among the mostly female salespeople that he soon suggested they complete their gift-buying elsewhere.

"You didn't seem too comfortable with all those women drooling over you," Nickie commented.

He groaned. "How would you have felt?"

Nickie laughed, but she felt a twinge of compassion for Jason. Women flocked to him like groupies to a rock star; it was something he just couldn't control. The question was, could she live with it? And trust him not to succumb?

"Well, it looks like you'll have great traffic in the store today," Nickie remarked as they continued on.

Jason nodded happily. "I spoke with Ed Simpson, my controller, yesterday, and he says that it looks like this year will be our best."

"Hey, Jason, that's great."

"Houston's on the rebound," he replied with a grin.

They moved through the stores, completing their purchases. Jason helped Nickie select gifts for members of her family—a box of salamis and cheeses for her mother and Steve, a peignoir set for Meredith to wear at the hospital and some expensive Scotch for Richard, as well as gifts for her brother, Mack, and his family. Jason bought little else, mentioning that he had already mailed presents to his mother and aunt. Guiltily, Nickie realized he would have no one to spend Christmas with.

While they were in the toy section of a department store, hunting for presents for Mack's children, they paused to watch the younger children line up to see Santa Claus. A photographer stood close by, snapping shots of each child on Santa's knee.

Jason playfully nudged Nickie toward the line. "Why don't you go tell Santa what you'd like for Christmas?"

"Jason, you nut!" she protested.

"I'd love to have a picture of you on Santa's lap," he went on, with a charming flash of his dimples. Then he wrapped an arm around her waist and wiggled his eyebrows devilishly. "On second thought, on my lap would be much better."

Nickie laughed and watched a toddler clamber onto Santa's knee, his little eyes filled with wonder as he solemnly tugged on Kris Kringle's beard. Her own expression grew pensive and wistful.

"What are you wishing for, Nickie?" Jason whispered in her ear, his breath warm on her earlobe. "Perhaps a few munchkins to take home with us?"

She looked up to meet his tenderly amused gaze, then turned away quickly as her own eyes misted with tears. She dared not say what she really wished for in that moment—for things to work out between them.

They grabbed a sandwich at Bennigan's, watched the skaters glide around the ice rink for a while, and then headed on to Jason's condo, where he was planning to cook them a traditional Christmas dinner.

Jason's condominium was on the twentieth floor of a posh high-rise off Post Oak. After they entered through the imposing double doors, Nickie stood at the edge of the foyer while Jason put away their jackets in the closet behind her. She found she was unprepared for her reaction to being in Jason's home again.

The living room beyond her was just as she remembered it—elegant and darkly masculine, with gray carpeting, black leather couch and chairs, walnut bookcases, marble fireplace and subdued track lighting. The small Christmas tree Jason had put up, along with the Christmas cards on the mantel, added festive touches. This was the place where she and Jason had lived together as man and wife.

Last Christmas, they'd been happy here. It hadn't all been anguish and heartache. Perhaps not until this moment had she realized how keenly she had missed the good times in their marriage.

Jason seemed to sense her bittersweet mood as he came to her side and laid a hand on her shoulder. "Remembering, Nickie?"

She nodded. "It's been a long time since I've been here."

He tilted her chin with his thumb and kissed her quickly. "Far too long," he pronounced solemnly. They stared at each other for an awkward moment. "Well—help me cook?"

"Sure."

Out in the kitchen, Jason fixed Nickie a Coke. She sipped her drink and mostly watched as he prepared stuffing for the turkey. He'd always been a marvelous cook, she recalled fondly. Standing on tiptoe, she peered over his shoulder, watching him chop celery and mushrooms. He'd rolled up the sleeves of his dark blue shirt, and she admired the fluid grace of his forearms as he worked. He smelled marvelous, too. Watching the light dance on his blond hair, she was strongly tempted to press her lips against the delightfully crisp curl at the nape of his neck.

She was about to succumb to temptation when Jason abruptly set down the knife and turned to her with a smile. "What's this? The Undercover Gourmet?"

She laughed, then squealed as he grabbed her, cola and all, and hoisted her onto the countertop flanking him.

"There, half-pint, now you can really see," he teased.

"You stinker." Wrinkling her nose at him, she tried to get down, but Jason forestalled her by plopping a cocktail shrimp into her mouth. This was followed by several chopped walnuts and a few fresh cranberries.

"Oh, this is yummy," Nickie said as she chewed.

"I'm fattening you up for the kill," he explained. Then he ran his hand wickedly up her pant leg and then under her sweater.

Nickie grabbed his errant hand through her sweater. "Jason!"

But he again stymied her by dropping another shrimp in her mouth, then a kiss from his lips. Nickie didn't know whether to try to swallow or to kiss him back—both were delectable.

Suddenly she became aware of his audacious hand at the waistband of her slacks. "That's enough, Romeo," she said breathlessly, shoving his hand away. "Get that bird in the oven. You know what they say about letting dressing sit."

He chuckled and went back to work, whistling a Christmas carol. Nickie continued to watch him, studying his beautiful hands as they moved with rhythmic precision, watching his Adonis-like features catch the light. With each passing moment, she grew more mesmerized by his physical beauty. When at last he carried their feast to the oven, *he* was her feast. She watched him bend over to set the roaster in the oven, watched the fabric of his trousers pull against his hard buttocks, and she almost moaned aloud. She tried to distract herself by glancing around the room, only to be swept by a wave of nostalgia as she spotted the canisters his aunt had given them as a wedding present, and the pot holders she'd bought. This was their home, the place where they'd once loved each other, however briefly. Now, they were still married, and it would be so easy to . . .

"Well." Having set the timer on the oven, Jason strode over to Nickie, dusting off his hands. "We're finished in here for now. While the turkey cooks, why don't we build a fire and watch a movie, half-pint?"

Nickie shook a finger at him. "Call me half-pint again, and I'll see that you live to regret it."

He only chuckled and caught her beneath the arms, lowering her slowly down the front of his body. For a moment, they stood pressed together. Looking up, Nickie caught the intense gleam in his eyes and her mouth went dry. She realized how very aroused he was—and how very aroused *she* was. She asked in a bright, if squeaky voice, "You said a movie?"

"And a fire," he added meaningfully, stroking the tip of her nose with his fingertip.

Nickie nodded and made a dash for the living room. Laughing, Jason followed her.

Nickie curled up in one corner of the couch and watched him build the fire. She again marveled at his physical beauty as he stacked the logs and started the kindling. This sexy, captivating man wanted to make love with her, wanted her to spend Christmas with him. What was wrong with her that she resisted him so? Why did she cling so tenaciously to her doubts? After all, Jason had revealed a new side of himself during past weeks—that of a caring man who seemed devoted to her and to making their relationship work. Why couldn't she simply *believe*, just like the children who had lined up to see Santa today?

The tantalizing scent of smoldering logs filled the room. Jason put a videotape in the VCR, then came over to the couch and sat down in the corner opposite Nickie. The reflection of the flames danced in his eyes as he grinned, saying, "You gonna hug that corner, woman? Or come over here and hug me?"

"Oh, Jason." Nickie melted on the spot. She began to crawl toward him, but he reached out and caught her under the arms, pulling her into his lap and kissing her. Then they both started as music blurted out on the VCR. Jason grabbed the remote control and turned down the volume, but by then, they were both distracted.

Nickie stared at the movie flashing onto the screen. *"It's a Wonderful Life,"* she said. "Hey, that's one of my favorites."

For a few moments, they sat curled up like two spoons, watching the film. But long before Jimmy Stewart's angel showed up to offer salvation, Nickie was beyond redemption, when Jason leaned over and pressed his lips on hers. Her heart beat so wildly in her ears that she could no longer hear the movie. She realized that being here, where they had loved before, was the most potent aphrodisiac of all. She reeled as Jason's tongue plunged into her mouth. His bold hands caught the hem of her sweater, and he tugged the soft cashmere off her before she could even protest. Then he rolled her body beneath his on the couch and stared down into her flushed face.

"You're so beautiful," he said reverently, stroking her hair.

"Jason, I'm not—"

"Yes, you are," he cut in intently. "With the fire reflected in those dark eyes and shining in your hair."

"Oh, Jason."

He caught her face in his hands and brought her lips up to his. She moaned, totally lost in the seductive magic of his kiss. His body felt so hard, so strong, so right against hers, and his erection pressed provocatively against her, making a near-painful yearning twist and spiral inside her.

As he undid the clasp of her bra, she pulled at the buttons on his shirt. "You're beautiful," she said, running her fingertips over the hard muscles of his chest, the crisp hair. "I couldn't take my eyes off you in the kitchen."

"I noticed," he said with a wry smile.

Jason nibbled on her earlobe, her neck, her shoulder. He drew back and stared down at her breasts, squeezing them with his hands. He smiled as she tossed her head and squirmed in pleasure. "Have I told you how much I love your breasts?" he asked, his voice sounding husky.

"I seem to recall your mentioning it in the throes of passion," she gasped.

"I love the way the nipples pucker when I tease them with my tongue," he murmured, and then paused to demonstrate on both her breasts, holding her fast when she practically came up off the couch.

"And furthermore," he continued, drawing his lips down to her stomach, "I just love your little body, darling."

Nickie thrust her hands wildly through his hair and gasped, "Jason, are we—er—going to—"

"Isn't it what we both want?" he asked intensely.

Oh, yes, Nickie thought. *Yes*. She was squirming like a woman lying on a bed of ants, and Jason was trying his best to unzip her slacks, when the timer in the kitchen went off.

"Damn!" he said, his head snapping up. "Time to baste the turkey."

Nickie laughed and ruffled his hair. "Saved by the bell."

"Wanna bet?" he growled.

After he left, she realized she was trembling all over. She donned her sweater and bra, grabbed her purse and retreated to an easy chair.

A moment later, Jason reappeared. She swallowed hard as she glimpsed him standing in the doorway, shirtless, with his hair rumpled, his belt unbuckled and that shuttered, sexy look in his eyes. Lord, he had never looked more irresistible!

A fierce glower knit his features as he spotted her in the chair. "Oh, no, you don't," he said in an ominous voice.

Nickie couldn't resist throwing him an impish smirk. Then, as he sprinted across the room, she made a frantic attempt to escape him but was too late. Laughing, he tackled her, hoisted her up into his arms, then wrestled her back down onto the couch with him.

Within ten seconds, her sweater and bra hit the floor and she was moaning. Nickie was unable to retrieve those items of clothing for some time as they kissed and caressed on the couch. However, minding the turkey kept them just short of consummation. Again and again, the frustrating ritual was repeated—kisses, heavy breathing and then the bell going off. Seduction amid turkey basting.

"I'm going to let the damn thing stew in its own juices," Jason grumbled the next time he got up.

"Now, Jason," Nickie purred, "you know you pride yourself on being a gourmet cook."

"And an epicurean lover," he added wickedly.

They were both in a breathless, aroused state by the time dinner was served. Nickie was practically squirming on her chair as they sat in the candlelit dining room eating the famous turkey. "It's wonderful," she managed to say, wishing it was Jason she was consuming.

And all through the meal, his eyes devoured her.

Then, with the coffee, he brought out a pumpkin pie and a small, foil-wrapped box. "Merry Christmas, Nickie," he said tenderly.

"Thanks, Jason," she murmured, fingering the velvet box. "Your present is still at my town house. Guess we'll have to get it when you take me home."

"Guess so," he said. "But open yours now—okay?"

She nodded, tugging at the bow. She unwrapped a small velvet jewelry case, then gasped as she opened it. Inside was a dazzling gold-capped diamond tennis bracelet. "Oh, Jason!"

"Oh, hush, and put it on," he said with a grin. He took the bracelet from the box and fastened it on her wrist. "See, it's perfect for you—lovely and precious." He leaned over and brushed her lips briefly with his. "Hey, hon, why don't we go for a drive and see the Christmas lights?"

Nickie fought to contain a twinge of disappointment. "Yes, that would be lovely."

"Why don't you go grab your jacket, and I'll finish up here?" he suggested.

"Sure."

She went out to the closet to get her coat. Opening the door, she was stunned when a huge white teddy bear popped out and practically knocked her over. "Jason! Help!" she cried.

Even as she frantically struggled with the enormous bear, she heard the sound of Jason's hearty laughter coming from behind her. She managed to turn and saw him standing nearby with a delighted grin on his face.

"I thought you'd enjoy something frivolous for Christmas, too, so I bought you Bear, here," he explained. "I remembered how you always loved plush animals."

Nickie was now staring eyeball-to-eyeball at the large button eyes on the bear's face. "Good grief, Jason! He wasn't in the closet when we got here."

He chuckled. "I know. I sneaked him into the closet while you were washing up for dinner."

Nickie looked in amazement at the large red bow tied around the bear's neck, and at his barrel chest and rounded belly. She giggled. "He's awfully cute, but he's so huge. What am I going to do with him?"

He shrugged. "Use your imagination. If I can't sleep with you, maybe you can cuddle up with him."

Nickie felt herself blushing. "I don't think I'd better pursue that loaded subject. Didn't you say you wanted to go look at Christmas lights?"

Laughing, the two of them donned their coats and struggled out the door with the enormous teddy. They placed Bear in the back seat of Jason's car, then settled themselves in the front.

"I feel a little silly," Nickie confessed, glancing back at the enormous plush animal. "But I should have known that if you ever gave me a bear, it would be a big one. A 'stellar bear,' I suppose."

He laughed. "'Stellar Bear.' Hey, I like the sound of that."

Jason drove them out to a subdivision in northwest Houston that one of his employees had suggested they see. While both Nickie and Jason had heard that this particular neighborhood went all out on Christmas decorations, neither was prepared for a virtual sea of lights and fabulous decorations. Neither of them minded the heavy Christmas Eve traffic, which allowed them to stare all the longer at the lights dripping from trees and out-lining houses and edging lawns.

"Jason, this is wonderful!" Nickie exclaimed. "I'm so glad you suggested we drive out here."

"I've never seen anything like it," he agreed.

Nickie felt as if they were totally a part of the magic—even Bear in the back seat seemed to belong.

Traffic in the subdivision grew so heavy that Jason suggested they park and walk a few blocks to get a closer look. Holding hands, they walked down a street where glittering mechanical figures and signs told the story of "The Night Before Christmas." The night air was cold and crisp; thousands of stars twinkled in the dark sky above them. Nickie mused that she had never felt happier than she did at this moment. Most of the homes they passed had their drapes pulled open to show their Christmas trees, and her heart welled at these images of family love and unity.

As they walked past a display of a Santa going down a chimney, Jason asked, "What did you wish for when you looked at Santa in the store today?"

Nickie glanced at him, startled. "What makes you think I made a wish?"

"The look in your eyes. You did make a wish, didn't you?"

"Yes." She suddenly felt shy. "Maybe I'll tell you—later."

"Tell me something now."

"Yes?"

He pulled her to a halt beneath a tree aglow with tiny white lights. Placing his hands on her shoulders, he asked seriously, "Why do you think I married you, Nickie?"

She bit her lip, unprepared for the direct question. "I guess I'm still not sure," she answered honestly.

"Oh, but you have your theories, don't you? I've been hearing enough of them, at the beach house—and since."

"Such as?"

"Such as my thinking that we made a good team, or my wanting to make an honest woman out of you, or my deciding to marry someone I wouldn't have to compete with."

"And none of that had a bearing?" she asked with a touch of sadness.

He was silent a moment. "Look out at all this splendor, Nickie. It's very spectacular. Very 'stellar,' as you would say. But think of all the work that was put into it, all the hours and heartache and backbreaking labor behind the scenes. Think of all the energy it takes to keep these displays going each night."

"It's an awesome prospect. But what's the point?"

He gazed down at her and spoke passionately. "The point is, Nickie, you're my energy, my stability. You're what holds my life together, what makes me shine. I don't want a Stephanie Stellar. Let's face it: Two 'stellar attractions' would only burn each other up."

Nickie felt deeply touched by his words, and she couldn't resist a small smile. "So I'm stable, huh?"

"You're my rock, Nickie," he said tenderly. "And nothing works in my life without you."

"Oh, Jason."

Jason pulled her into his arms and kissed her then. The lights shimmering above them couldn't compare with the brilliance dancing along Nickie's nerve endings. They stayed there, mouths locked together, until a passing carload of teenagers hooted catcalls at them. Then they laughed and headed back to his car.

Their walk in the cold air had been chilling, yet Nickie felt as if she were burning up with fever as she drove off with Jason. Staring at him seated across from her, she realized that over the past weeks, she had been seduced, irrevocably seduced. She had fallen in love again. And Jason's words of reassurance just now had utterly melted her. She loved the image of him as the lights and her as the energy that made the lights work. Right now, it was all she could do not to climb all over him.

Soon they were parked before her town house. They laughed as they struggled up the path with Stellar Bear between them. At the door, Nickie said brightly, "Now you have to come in and get your Christmas present."

Suddenly nervous, she said, "We can have a Christmas toast." Then she hastily amended. "Oh, I forgot, you don't drink anymore. You know, you really have changed in a lot of ways, Jason."

His eyes lit up at her words. "You don't know how thrilled I am to hear you say that." Catching her close, he added tenderly, "I don't need a drink, Nickie. You're my Christmas toast. You're sweeter than any champagne."

"Oh, Jason."

Even as his words made her heart soar, he leaned over and crushed her lips against his in a long, thorough kiss. "Now tell me what you wished for today," he whispered.

Staring up into his impassioned eyes, she realized that nothing but the truth would do at this moment. "I wished that everything would work out—really work out—between us," she said in a choked voice.

"Oh, love."

This time Nickie pressed her lips on Jason's, kissing him with all her heart. He reached for her hand, taking her house key and turning it in the lock. A moment later, the three of them—Jason, Bear and Nickie—practically crashed into her front foyer.

Laughing as she wobbled on her feet, Nickie reached for the light switch.

Jason restrained her hand. "No, don't turn on the lights," he whispered urgently. He flipped the bolt on the lock, then pulled her tightly against him again. "Still want to move away from me, Nickie?"

They stood there with bodies locked, need pressed to throbbing need, and she was again choked with tears. "No, I don't want to move away from you. I want you, Jason. Now."

"Darling, you've got me."

Moving so fast he made her head spin, Jason backed her into the tiny alcove to the right of the door. He lifted her onto the shelf, settling her between the ficus and the fern, and kissed her hungrily.

Nickie's heart thumped in a wanton, crazy rhythm. She realized he intended to make love to her right here, right now. Of course—she had said "now." The realization sent desire rocketing through her body like exploding fireworks.

It felt wonderful and illicit, with him tearing off her bra and slacks. To their left was a bottled-glass panel, with moonlight spilling through. Nickie knew no one could actually see them through the thick, distorted glass, but still, the setting seemed wicked, risqué.

"Delicious," he murmured as his lips sank into her breast.

She panted with excitement and pressed her breast greedily into the wet heat of his mouth. It seemed like an eternity since they had loved each other, and she was suddenly consumed by an urgency that matched his. She tore open his shirt, sending the buttons flying, then ran her hands eagerly over his bare, muscular chest. He groaned as his impatient fingers slipped inside her panties, digging into her bottom. She felt the silky fabric sliding past her knees, to the floor. And then his mouth—

"Jason," she gasped. "You're knocking me off my feet."

But he only laughed. "That's the idea, darling." He insinuated a hand between her thighs, stroking boldly upward with his fingers as his mouth continued its magic. The pleasure grew too intense, making Nickie's head buzz. She tried to wriggle away, but succeeded only in deepening the pressure of Jason's penetrating fingers, even as his mouth and tongue moved with deliberate gentleness. A hot riot of ecstasy flooded her senses.

"Jason!" He heard the urgency in her voice, and in an instant he was standing close to her. Impatiently, she undid his trousers and slipped her hand inside his briefs, stroking him provocatively. The size and hardness of him took her breath away. "Now, Jason, please," she whimpered, tugging down his briefs.

He lifted her onto him and let her slide down onto his erect shaft ever so slowly. Going insane by inches at the sweet torture, she clawed at his back and bit his shoulder. He chuckled at her impatience. "Easy, darling. Hold on tight and I'll give you everything you want."

He did, pressing her against the wall and possessing her utterly. Nickie cried out; the magnitude of him inside her was exquisite, yet she eagerly wrapped her legs around his waist, welcoming all the love and passion his body could pour out. Arching into Jason's thrusts, Nickie soared, her entire being focused on the tension building and knotting inside her. With hoarse love words, she urged Jason on, until he was thundering toward release. Then the force of her own climax swamped her; her fingers uncoiled against his chest and she heard him groan as he followed her to rapture.

Afterward, they clung together for a long moment, kissing deeply as their bodies gradually relaxed and their breathing returned to normal.

"You okay?" he asked.

"Oh, yes," she whispered.

Chuckling, he set her gently on her feet. He draped his shirt about her shoulders before he switched on the light.

She blinked in the brightness, and then her heart skidded as she stared at him. There was lipstick on his face and his half-zipped slacks clung to his hips.

He leaned over and righted the plant they'd spilled, then quipped, "Love on a shelf."

"Passion in bloom." With a giggle, she added, "We forgot about your present."

"Oh, no, we didn't."

She shivered as a draft wafted through a crack in the door and sent goose bumps up her bare legs. "Want some hot chocolate or something? I mean, I did promise you a drink—"

"Hey, you're trembling, Nickie," he cut in. "Why don't we take a nice hot bath, then we can have some cocoa afterward?"

She flashed him a crooked smile. "Do you want a wash or a ravishment?"

"What do you think?"

Jason moved against her brazenly, then they both dashed upstairs, laughing and tearing at each other's clothes.

SOMETIME DURING the passion-filled night, she remembered Jason's present. He modeled the new leather bomber jacket for her, wearing it with just his briefs and a silly grin. She collapsed in gales of laughter, calling out, "Take it off!" And he did.

Sometime during the passion-filled night, she also remembered that they'd done nothing about birth control. She sat up in bed and gasped, "Good grief, my diaphragm!" Jason stumbled over to the dresser and she watched, amused, as he rifled through her jewelry box. "You're not going to find my diaphragm in there, Romeo!" she called out.

Jason returned to the bed and slipped her wedding rings onto her finger. "These are all you need to wear when you make love to me," he said tenderly, and Nickie began to cry, throwing her arms about him.

The rings were all she wore for the rest of that passion-filled night.

10

AT NOON ON CHRISTMAS DAY, Nickie awakened to a
ringing phone. She jumped, then quickly realized that
she was securely entangled in Jason's arms and legs. The
phone trilled again. Reaching for it, she encountered the
awesome bulk of Stellar Bear. The huge plush animal was
solidly wedged between her body and the nightstand.
Her face flamed as she remembered Jason bringing the
bear to bed in the middle of the night, and how they'd
joked about a ménage à trois.

After the third ring, Nickie somehow managed to
reach over Stellar Bear and pick up the phone. "Hello?"

"Nickie, where in the heck are you?" came Meredith's
impatient voice. "We've all been at Mom's for hours, and
Christmas dinner is almost ready."

Nickie glanced, crestfallen, at the clock. "Oh, Lord,
I'm sorry, Mere," she said, running a hand through her
disheveled hair. "I overslept."

"I figured as much. Look—get your clothes on and get
over here ASAP, okay?"

"Sure, Mere, I'll hurry. But tell Mom not to hold dinner."

"Of course, we'll hold dinner. You know how Mom
insists on having everyone together at Christmas."

Nickie sighed. "Okay. See you soon. Give Mom my
apologies—and Merry Christmas."

"Merry Christmas to you, kid. Now, hurry."

Nickie hung up the phone, and her eyes met Jason's. He was lying with his chin propped in his hand, watching her solemnly. Just the sight of him made her pulse race with excitement. She managed a weak smile. "Good morning. Merry Christmas."

"Good morning and Merry Christmas to you," he said.

Jason pressed her back into the pillows and kissed her, flicking his fingertips sensually over her bare breast. Feeling herself about to slip back into the world of sexual abandon, Nickie pushed against his chest. "Jason, that was my sister."

He chuckled. "So I surmised."

Feeling miserable, she continued, "I've got to go. The family's holding Christmas dinner for me."

Abruptly he rolled away from her. "Okay, then," he said tightly. "You'd best hurry."

Feeling guilty, Nickie climbed out of bed. She felt a slight twinge of soreness between her thighs as she reached for her robe. The tenderness of her body, as well as the heat of Jason's gaze on her as she headed for the bathroom, was a potent reminder of their fevered lovemaking of the night before.

When she hurried to the bedroom dresser to select her underclothes, Nickie could still feel the force of Jason's gaze on her. Otherwise, the two of them dressed in strained silence. She desperately wished she had more time—time to sort out her feelings, her options; time to try to explain things to him. She knew that what was hanging in the air between them was the fact that she hadn't asked him to accompany her to her mother's. In light of her behavior last night, she'd surely be a hypocrite if she didn't ask him along; yet she still wasn't quite ready to announce to her family, much less to herself, that the two of them were firmly reconciled.

Nickie actually felt relieved when Jason left the room to hunt for his shirt. While he was gone, she hurriedly finished dressing, donning a black wool skirt and a red sweater. He returned momentarily with his shirt on but unbuttoned. He held out the buttons in one hand and flashed her a lame smile. "Hon, I think I've got a problem here."

Nickie couldn't repress a laugh at his helpless expression, even as she blushed at the memory of herself wantonly tearing at his shirt. Now, he looked so adorably bewildered that she wanted to grab him and kiss him senseless. Instead, she quickly detoured to the dresser and found her sewing kit. As she hunted for the right color of thread, he offered to try to sew the buttons on himself, but she firmly refused.

She sat on the bed, hastily sewing, while he sat next to her, shirtless, watching her. Having him so near—not to mention half-dressed—made her flustered and self-conscious, and she jabbed herself with the needle. When she muttered, "Ouch!" he took her hand and kissed the wounded finger. "Easy, Nickie. It's okay."

Seeing his compassionate expression, Nickie bit her lip to hold back tears. He should be furious at her for deserting him this way; instead, he was being wonderful. She quickly returned her attention to the sewing, and didn't draw a comfortable breath until she had finished.

At last they faced each other across the room, both fully clothed. "Jason . . ." she began helplessly.

He stood at the dresser, stuffing his wallet into his back pocket. "Call me later?" he asked.

The fact that he looked so lost, combined with the fact that he still hadn't pushed her, was Nickie's undoing. She flew into his arms, hugging him tightly. "Jason, please come with me to Mom's house."

His eyes lit with joy. "Nickie, are you sure?"

She nodded. "Christmas is a time for families to be together. I want my family complete today." Her voice broke as she added, "And it won't be complete without you."

"Oh, Nickie" She spotted tears in Jason's eyes as his mouth swiftly took hers.

FIFTEEN MINUTES LATER, they were in Jason's car driving toward her mother's. The back seat was crammed with the presents Nickie had bought for her family, and she was glad that she'd taken a moment to add Jason's name to the gift tags before they left.

Studying Jason seated beside her, she had to smile. The disposable razor she'd found for him either hadn't agreed with him or he'd shaved much too quickly—and a thin red scratch marred the usual perfection of his strong jaw. Bless his heart, when she'd suggested that they stop at his condominium so he could shower and change, he had refused, in deference to her mom. At least he'd worn the new leather jacket she'd given him. Still, she had to admit that there was a thrown-together air to both their appearances, given their haste to depart.

Given their haste . . . She thought of their haste making love last night, and wondered if she'd lost her mind. What had happened to her firm conviction not to sleep with Jason again until she was certain that they could make it as a married couple?

Christmas had happened, she thought ruefully. Magic had happened. Falling in love again had happened. She had plotted her course with her intellect and had been shanghaied by her emotions. Now, not only had she

abandoned her better judgment and gone to bed with
Jason too soon, but they had also made love three—no,
four—times without birth control. Now she was taking
Jason home with her to the family gathering, and everyone was bound to think they had reconciled.

Hadn't they? She stared at the wedding rings Jason had
slipped back onto her finger last night, and the new diamond bracelet on her wrist; all were outward symbols
of marital commitment. And Nickie had seen solid evidence that Jason had changed. But she still didn't feel
certain that the old problems wouldn't reemerge to destroy their relationship once again—Jason's drinking, his
obsession with work. And she still wasn't sure that she
could ever trust him completely around other women.

Should she have believed his words in the moonlight
last night? Could she really satisfy this "stellar attraction" for a lifetime?

SITTING ACROSS FROM Nickie, Jason also felt troubled.
Last night had been paradise; he had felt so close to
Nickie in every way. And when she made love to him, he
had felt certain that she was signaling a renewed commitment to their relationship. He'd been thrilled that
she'd asked him along to the family gathering today. But
now that they were on their way, he could sense that her
fears were resurfacing, coming between them again.
Why did she so easily doubt their love? Why couldn't she
trust him?

She was so open and giving in bed. He stifled a groan
as he remembered their making love shortly before
dawn—how eagerly she'd wrapped her legs about his
waist and taken him deeply inside her. She never held
back when they made love and refused to allow him to

do so. Why couldn't she take that same trusting openness outside the bedroom?

As he stopped the car at a light, he reached over and took her hand, squeezing it tightly and smiling at her. *Give us a chance, Nickie,* his eyes implored. *Please give us a chance.*

Sitting across from Jason, Nickie squeezed his hand in response and met his gaze. Despite all her doubts, she was momentarily lost in his tender smile and the beseeching quality in his eyes. She loved him so, she thought achingly. She just loved him so....

Moments later, they arrived at Vivian Miller's. The day was bright and cold; a brisk wind bent the azalea plants that lined the sidewalk. With their arms bursting with presents, Nickie and Jason rushed onto the porch of the one-story Colonial house. As Jason rang the bell, Nickie glanced through the sheer curtains into the living room. She spotted the huge Christmas tree aglow with lights, its skirt heaped with colorfully wrapped presents.

Their ring was promptly answered by Steve Miller, Nickie's stepdad. He was a giant bear of a man with a broad smile and booming voice. "Nickie!" he cried, hugging her. "And Jason—how good to see the two of you together again! Now, come right in, and let me help you with those boxes."

They stepped into the terrazzo-floored foyer, and Nickie reveled in the familiar scents of home and Christmas—the pine of the tree, the delicious aromas of bread and turkey baking, and the tantalizing, tangy smell of hot wassail. Steve took the boxes from Nickie's arms and bellowed out, "Vivian! Come look who's here!"

While Steve went off to place the presents under the tree, Nickie's mother rushed into the room with eyes aglow. Vivian Miller was a petite, graying version of her daughter; today, in honor of the occasion, she wore a cream-colored silk blouse and a festive green velvet, floor-length skirt. "Why, Nickie—and Jason, too! What a wonderful surprise to have you both here!"

"Merry Christmas, Mom!" Nickie said, hugging her mother tightly. "I'm sorry we're so late."

Vivian waved her off. "Oh, don't give it a thought. We're delighted to have you."

"Merry Christmas, Vivian," Jason added, leaning over to kiss her cheek. "I hope it's no imposition that I've—"

"Now, don't you dare say it, Jason!" she scolded. "You're family, for heaven's sake." Vivian wrapped an arm around each of their waists. "Oh, I'm so excited I could just burst! I can't tell you how thrilled I am to see the two of you together again—especially at Christmas. Now, let me take your jackets, then we'll get you something hot to drink."

Vivian had just left to put away their coats, and Jason had gone into the living room to deposit the rest of their presents under the tree, when Nickie heard two excited, familiar young voices trill out, "Aunt Nickie, Aunt Nickie!"

Nickie whirled in delight, watching her brother's twin four-year-old boys, Kevin and Devin, come rushing into the foyer. Dark-haired and dark-eyed, the twins were adorable balls of fire.

The boys descended on her, grabbing her around the legs and almost knocking her over. "Santa came and brought us a Nintendo game!" Kevin cried gleefully, his eyes bright with excitement as he stared up at his aunt.

"And monster trucks!" Devin added.

"Did you bring us a present, Aunt Nickie?" Kevin asked wistfully.

"I sure did," she replied, fondly ruffling his hair.

"Where are your glasses, Aunt Nickie?" Devin added, squinting up at her.

Before Nickie could answer, Kevin spotted Jason at the Christmas tree. "Uncle Jason!" he cried, and the twin whirling dervishes dashed off to confront Jason with their myriad questions. With a grin, Jason hefted both boys into his arms and answered each of their queries solemnly.

Nickie was chuckling at the sight when she heard her brother, Mack, speaking behind her. "Nickie, great to see you, kid!"

Nickie turned to him. Like his younger sister, Mack Smith was short and dark, but was also developing a decided paunch and thinning hair. "Mack, it's been too long," she said, giving him a warm hug. "How are things in Dallas?"

"Great. I just got promoted to purchasing manager at the hospital."

"Hey, congratulations," Nickie said, playfully punching him in the arm.

Mack laughed ruefully. "My raise came just in time for Santa. We'll be needing the extra dough with all these mouths to feed."

"Speaking of which, where are Miriam and my niece?"

"Miriam's changing Jenny," Mack said. In a lower voice, he confided, "The toilet training isn't going quite as well as planned." As she giggled, he glanced across the room and spotted Jason with the twins. He shot his sister an amazed look. "You two back together?"

"Well," Nickie hedged, "not exactly. It's kind of a long story—"

"Uh-huh," he said with a grave nod. "Think I'll go say hello." Walking off, he called out, "Hey, Jason, good to see you."

Nickie stood watching the two men shake hands, then turned toward the den just as Meredith emerged, wearing a voluminous green maternity dress. "Nickie! Well, it's about time, kid!"

Nickie gazed at her sister in astonishment, her mouth falling as she observed how much larger Meredith's stomach had grown since she last saw her. Her sister was *huge*—there was simply no other word for it. She was obviously in the final stage of pregnancy.

Nickie stepped forward and hugged Meredith gingerly. "Mere, good grief. You look as if you're going to have that baby any minute. Are you sure you should be on your feet right now?"

Meredith tossed her long, ash-blond curls. "Honey, at this stage, there's no comfortable position, believe me." As Nickie laughed, Meredith examined her younger sister more closely. "Hey, the contacts look great. Was I right?"

Nickie nodded and smiled. "You were. Thanks again, Mere."

"You're most welcome."

Meredith's husband, Richard, joined them in the foyer, handing each sister a cup of hot wassail. "Hi, Nickie. I keep telling Meredith that we may get our tax deduction this year, after all."

Nickie laughed. She liked Meredith's husband. Richard wasn't fabulously handsome, but he was affable and kind, and he adored Meredith. And while Richard was a highly successful tax attorney, he was also very down to earth, constantly joking about ways he and Meredith could save on their taxes. Nickie knew quite well, however, that nothing mattered more to Richard than the welfare of Meredith and their child.

Jason now sauntered over to join them, prompting an amazed glance from Meredith. He kissed his sister-in-law on the cheek and shook Richard's hand. "Good to see you folks again."

Meredith turned to Nickie with avid curiosity. "You two back together?"

Nickie felt her face flame as all eyes were suddenly focused on her. Yet she was spared the need to reply as Jason hooked an arm around her neck, ducked to kiss her quickly on the lips, then announced proudly, "We sure the heck are."

"So that's why you were late," Meredith said, elbowing Nickie and grinning slyly.

The blush on Nickie's face deepened as Meredith and Richard offered their congratulations. Nickie thought of issuing a denial—but then, what could she say? "Well, folks, even though I spent all last night attacking Jason like some tigress in heat, I'm just not sure about our relationship...."

Before Nickie could speak, Meredith spotted the diamond bracelet on Nickie's wrist and whistled. "Hey, nice set of rocks, kiddo."

"Jason gave me the bracelet for Christmas," Nickie explained with acute embarrassment.

"And I see you're wearing your wedding rings again, as well." Meredith slanted Richard a meaningful glance. "Things are looking serious."

At this critical juncture, Nickie's mother joined them, handing Jason a cup of wassail and rescuing Nickie from the uncomfortable moment. "I'll have soup for everyone in a moment," Vivian announced cheerfully as she headed back for the kitchen.

After she left, Jason curled an arm around Nickie's waist and winked at Meredith. "Hey, sis, are you going to give us a demonstration of birthing procedures for dessert?"

"Jason, you have a dirty mind, as always," Meredith teased back, as Richard laughed.

Jason feigned amazement. "A dirty mind? Why, there's nothing at all shameful about childbirth." He drew Nickie closer and added, "Give Nickie and me another year and we'll prove it to you."

"Jason!" Mortified, Nickie tried to shove him away, but he only drew her possessively closer again, keeping her bound to his side as they continued chatting with Meredith and Richard.

VIVIAN SERVED THE FIRST course informally, setting out festive red and green mugs filled with hot clam chowder. The entire clan visited in the kitchen and den as they sipped the delicious soup. Jason and Steve stoked the fire in the den while Nickie helped her mother and sister-in-law, Miriam, put the finishing touches on the meal. By now, the air was redolent with irresistible aromas.

Mack's wife, Miriam, was petite, blond and cute, as was their daughter, Jenny. The two-year-old dashed among the women's skirts, handing out potholders and chattering incessantly.

"Nickie, I can't tell you how happy Mack and I are to see you and Jason back together," Miriam remarked as she sliced hot bread.

"Amen," Vivian added from the stove.

Nickie flashed the two other women a tentative smile. "Thanks for the good wishes. I just think I should tell you both that this is only a trial reconciliation."

"It looks like a lot more than a trial to me," Miriam remarked, nudging Nickie playfully. "Looks to me like the jury's back and the verdict is in—happily ever after."

"Happily ever after!" young Jenny chirped as she dashed by with a toss of her blond ponytail and a flounce of her red velvet skirt. The three women convulsed in laughter.

Nickie was still chuckling when Jason came up behind her and solidly locked both his forearms around her neck. "Need some help, hon?" he asked, moving his lips playfully against her ear.

While Vivian and Miriam exchanged meaningful glances, Nickie fought a shudder. "Jason, I can't work with you hanging on me like this."

"Oh, I don't need any more help," Vivian put in brightly.

Nickie tossed her mother a bemused look. Vivian had taken to Jason immediately, for reasons Nickie couldn't fathom. Nickie would have thought that her mom would be more cautious about her son-in-law, after having been married to a man who was so much like Jason.

Jason snuggled her even closer to his solid frame. Embarrassed, Nickie twisted in Jason's arms. "May I have a word with you, sir?"

"Of course, ma'am," he returned innocently.

She tugged Jason off to the utility room behind the kitchen and shut the door. "Jason, I want you to stop embarrassing me in front of my family."

"Embarrassing you? Am I embarrassing you?"

"Cut the innocent act, mister. It's downright disgraceful, the way you keep mauling me—not to mention, telling Richard and Meredith that we're back together."

"And aren't we back together?" he challenged, suddenly deadly serious.

She clenched her fists miserably, and her guilty eyes wouldn't meet his. "Jason, I'm just—not ready to make an announcement yet."

Jason pressed her against the washing machine. He caught her chin in his hand and forced her to look him in the eye. "Meaning that you're committed to me in bed but not out?"

Growing unstrung by his nearness, Nickie blurted, "Jason, that's not fair. I mean, it's not what I meant to say—"

"Nickie, you're my wife, and I don't give a damn if the whole world knows I can't keep my hands off you."

He demonstrated that point, kissing her as he curled his hand possessively over her breast. Further protests on her part soon became lost in whimpers of pleasure.

By the time they left the utility room, Nickie's face was very red and her resolve was in tatters.

SOON, EVERYONE gathered at the huge, linen-draped table in the dining room. Nickie and Jason sat together toward the middle. Once Steve and Vivian had taken their places at either end, Nickie's mother shocked her by asking her to say grace. She looked around the table and found ten pairs of eyes focused straight on her. Her gaze met Jason's and he winked at her and squeezed her hand. Suddenly she forgot all their problems and was simply glad that he was there, sharing Christmas with her. She realized that of all the people at the table, he meant the most. That knowledge both scared and warmed her, bringing a lump to her throat and a tear to her eye.

And she knew it was high time she said something to her family about the fact that she and Jason were here together. Thus, clearing her throat, she glanced around the table and began bravely, "I just wanted all of you to

know that Jason and I . . . Well, we've decided to discuss
things."

To her horror and delight, everyone clapped, even little Jenny. Nickie became so flustered by all the attention
that she was supremely grateful when Steve stepped in
and rescued her, offering to return thanks himself. When
he said sincerely, "Lord, thank you for bringing our entire family back together again," she and Jason shared a
special smile.

AFTER DINNER, everyone gathered in the living room to
drink coffee and open the presents the children hadn't
already devoured early that morning. Seating was lim-
ited, and spotting a vacant easy chair, Jason took Nickie's hand and announced, "Nickie can sit in my lap."

Amid snickers from the others, Nickie blushed and
said primly, "I'll sit on the arm of the chair."

She proceeded to do just that, and Jason quickly
hooked an arm about her waist and pulled her down into
his lap, prompting gales of laughter from everyone else.

She soon realized, to her mortification, that Jason was
aroused, his erection pressing against her bottom. And,
appalled though she was, fight it though she did, she became aroused, too. She thought she would die as the
family went through the endless ritual of present-opening
and small talk. Nickie's frustration level escalated as each
gift was unwrapped.

Yet, while she watched her niece and nephews tear into
their presents, all she could think of was how much she
longed for a child—Jason's child. Jason's arms tightened
about her waist, almost as if he had guessed her errant
thoughts.

FINALLY IT WAS TIME to leave. Alone with him in the car, she vented her frustration. "Jason, don't you ever do that again!"

"Did I do something to offend you?" he asked innocently.

"You absolutely humiliated me! First, hanging on me all the time—"

"But your shoulders are such an irresistible shelf, darling. The perfect height for propping my arms—"

"And then you became aroused in the presence of six adults, three small children and one innocent baby about to be born!"

Jason howled with laughter. "Don't blow a fuse, Nickie. You're the only one who noticed I was aroused—and the only one who counts, as far as that is concerned."

"Jason, I'm going to strangle you!"

"No, you're not. And why don't you just admit that the reason you're so angry is that you got pretty hot, too." He flashed her a positively depraved smile. "But don't worry. I'm the only one who noticed—and the only one who counts there, too."

"Why, of all the arrogant, obnoxious..." Nickie fumed in silence, until she realized Jason had driven onto a narrow lane that led into the park. He pulled off the road and stopped under the nearest tree. She caught her breath when she saw the naked need in his eyes. He pulled her toward him, his mouth colliding squarely with hers. Her cry of outrage became lost in his wild, brazen kiss. Holding her seething body captive, Jason ran his tongue over her lips, her teeth, and deep into her mouth, in a blatant dance of possession that soon had her toes curling.

Somehow she managed to wrench her lips free. "Jason, I'm mad at you. Don't you dare kiss me. Don't you dare—"

Further speech was again smothered by his lips. This time, he pulled her into his lap, hooking an elbow behind her neck and grinding his mouth into hers. As they wrestled, her jacket came unsnapped and her skirt twisted up around her hips, and when he slid his free hand high on one thigh to restrain her, she felt as if she'd just been seared by a brand. Her breasts began to throb against the crushing pressure of his chest, and an enervating heat radiated deep in her belly. All at once, the rage in her receded and all she could think of was how much she did desire him. He was right: She *was* aroused—aroused to fever pitch—and damned angry at herself because she couldn't resist him.

By the time the kiss ended, her lips were throbbing and she was in a half-dazed state. He cuddled her against his chest, and both of them took a moment to calm their ragged breathing and racing hearts. Nickie heard the distant hooting of an owl and the rustling of tree branches above them; both added to the romantic ambience of the night.

"Still mad at me?" he asked after a moment, running his hand through her hair.

"You're impossible," she said.

"And you wouldn't have me any other way."

She sighed. "You're probably right."

"Today was wonderful, wasn't it?"

She turned to look at him. "Yes, it was. Having the family together meant so much, but the best part was watching the children experience the wonder of Christmas."

His expression was suddenly wistful. "I've never really had a family—at least, not like you have. No brothers or sisters."

"I know." She started to add that she could be his family, but the words wouldn't quite make it past her lips.

"You know, we could have it all, Nickie" he continued, stroking her breast through her sweater. "Home, hearth, babies—"

"Jason, you're trying to seduce me again," she protested in a quavering voice.

"I love you, Nickie," he said tenderly.

That did it. With an incoherent whimper, Nickie kissed him. His hands were bold and industrious, slipping under her sweater, unhooking her bra. She moaned, taking his lips ravenously as he caressed each breast slowly and thoroughly. She kneaded his taut shoulder muscles with her fingertips and kissed the beautiful contours of his jaw, brushing her lips down his magnificent neck and unzipping his leather jacket. He reached for the waistband of her skirt, undoing the button and pulling down the zipper. His fingers slid beneath her half-slip, and then he found the spot, stroking her through her panties and panty hose. Nickie arched out of his lap, uttering a low cry as her hipbone impacted the steering wheel. Jason caught her back firmly against him and continued the torture. A moment later, he pressed the release on his seat, and they both slid back into the delicious darkness.

"Nickie, touch me," he begged hoarsely.

"You're going to get us arrested," she groaned. But she complied, rearranging herself on his lap, straddling him so she could reach his zipper. He moaned as she freed his penis and stroked him boldly, her fingers moving with seductive skill, up and down the distended shaft, and lower. When his fingers slid inside her panty hose to touch her more intimately, she uttered a wild cry and lurched forward, kissing him hungrily and pulling at his shirt.

A moment later, he chuckled. "Nickie, you just ripped off all the buttons you so painstakingly sewed on this morning."

She leaned over to nuzzle his bare chest. "Ah—but why do you think I used a single thread instead of a double? I want to be able to unwrap my treat at will."

He laughed his delight. "You women have Machiavellian minds." He stroked her in a particularly erotic manner that made her cry out again.

They aroused each other to razor-honed readiness. Starting to tug down her underclothes, Jason paused to laugh as he realized that her knees were firmly wedged on either side of him, soundly defeating his purpose. "Uh, hon, we seem to be having a logistical difficulty here...."

Nickie giggled. "Logistical difficulties have never stopped you before."

"Quite true." She heard the rip of her panties as he pulled her tighter against him. "Darling, feel free to be my guest at our January lingerie sale," he murmured, then sank himself to the hilt inside her.

Nickie caught a sharp, ecstatic breath. The feel of him, so deep and tight inside her, was incredibly delightful. "Oh, Jason!"

His teeth nibbled her shoulder. "Feel good?"

She moved her hips provocatively against him. "Wonderful."

He kissed the corner of her mouth and said huskily, "I fantasized making love to you like this while we were sitting there together today. Did you?"

She shuddered, electrified that their thoughts had been the same. "Yes."

"I looked at your nephews and niece, and dreamed of having a baby with you. Did you dream it, too?"

Tears stung her eyes as she said huskily, "Yes."

Nibbling on her jaw, he continued, "It meant so much to me last night, that you would risk getting pregnant—"

"Jason, you wouldn't let me—"

"I know you when you're determined, Nickie. You risked it."

"Okay, I risked it," she panted with desperation. "I want to risk it now. Just hush and love me."

The hoarse tone of pleading in her voice excited Jason so that he feared he would climax right then and there. He tried to hold back for her sake, but promptly lost control as she moved wantonly against him. Then Jason's release came with consuming force, and when he grasped Nickie's hips and moved even deeper inside her, she cried out and jerked backward, producing a loud wail from the car horn. She stiffened in surprise and Jason murmured, "Easy, darling," pulling her firmly back to him, locking her in his lap as they finished climaxing together. When it was over, he cradled her against him in the darkness, kissing her hair and face as she clung to him, breathless and trembling.

After a while she heard his husky chuckle. "How do you feel?"

"Like a naughty teenager."

"I've heard of bells ringing, but a car horn . . . You're the limit, darling. Although I must admit that last move really did the trick for me."

She laughed. "So I noticed. But, frankly, I remain stunned that the park ranger hasn't come by to haul us off to the calaboose."

Jason stared about the car. "I doubt he'd be able to see anything through the fogged-up windows. Besides, you forget that it's Christmas, darling. . . . 'Goodwill toward men.'"

She stroked him and smiled as he sprang robustly back to life. "So, has this man had enough goodwill for one night?"

"Not on your life," he growled, kissing her.

"Can't you keep your hands off me until we get home?" she muttered, and then she forgot all about talking. . . .

THEY SPENT THE REST of the holidays together, stealing every moment they could spare to be alone. Jason bought Nickie new lingerie, and she insisted on buying him a new shirt. She doubled over with laughter when he solemnly asked the store clerk, "Do you have anything in your executive line with snaps?"

Early on New Year's Day, they were fast asleep at Nickie's town house when the phone again rang. Nickie groggily grabbed the receiver and mouthed a hello.

"Hello, Aunt Nickie," came Richard's jubilant voice.

Nickie sat bolt upright in bed. "Mere had the baby!"

"She sure did. A healthy eight-pound, six-ounce boy."

"Oh, Richard, congratulations. How's Meredith?"

"Fine—and asking for her sister."

"We'll be right there."

Nickie hung up the phone and her eyes met Jason's. "Mere had a boy, and mother and son are fine," she announced exultantly.

"I'm so happy, darling," he replied. "Tell you what— you flip the flapjacks and I'll hitch up the buggy."

Nickie grabbed him and laughed until she cried.

At the hospital, they went first to Meredith's room. Steve and Vivian were already there, proudly visiting with Richard and Meredith.

"Nick, you're not going to believe this," Meredith announced brightly from her bed. "Richard and I had the first baby of the New Year!"

"Oh, Mere, I'm so happy for you!" Nickie cried, hugging her sister. "And you look absolutely radiant."

Richard showed everyone the early-morning edition of a local paper, with a picture of Meredith and the baby prominently displayed on the front page. "There'll be no fooling the IRS now," he grumbled, and everyone laughed.

Soon afterward, Jason and Nickie trekked down to the nursery. Nickie's eyes were filled with wonder as she stared at her tiny, dark-haired nephew; the infant was yawning and stretching in his bassinet. She stared up at Jason, who stood behind her. "Oh, Jason he's so tiny, so adorable and helpless. And look at all that hair!"

"Want to try for the first baby of the next New Year?" he asked tenderly, pressing his cheek to hers.

Nickie looked back at the precious baby and felt a lump in her throat. She couldn't help herself. She nestled more snugly against Jason and drew his arms tightly about her waist.

11

OVER THE NEXT COUPLE of weeks, Nickie and Jason spent almost every night in each other's arms. While they didn't actually move back in together, Nickie found herself unable to resist Jason sexually; indeed, she lacked any self-control as far as their physical relationship was concerned. She knew that emotionally, she was far from completely committed to him, still fearing that the same problems might resurface to test their marriage again. For this reason, she tried to use birth control—at least on those occasions when Jason could be persuaded to keep his hands off her long enough for her to go to the bathroom for her diaphragm. Still, every time she went to visit Meredith and saw the tiny miracle of her new baby nephew, she felt tempted—so tempted.

Nevertheless, soon after Christmas, there were changes that reinforced Nickie's doubts. For one thing, both she and Jason became much busier, and as a result, more stressed. Nickie couldn't forget that the same sort of climate had contributed to their first breakup.

The Galveston store in particular was consuming more of their lives as the opening approached. Nickie spent much of her free time helping Jason select the staff and set up the operations. On the one hand, she felt less threatened by the opening of this new store, since Jason was giving it more of a "down-home, small-town" feel—a change from the glitz of his other establishments. But helping him did take time away from her increasing tax load at work, and she couldn't shake her nagging fear that he might be using her.

That fear came to a head on an evening in mid-January. Jason had invited Nickie over to his condo, promising to cook her dinner if she would help him belatedly put away the Christmas decorations.

While they worked in the living room that night, packing away the ornaments in boxes, Nickie noted that Jason seemed unusually tense. He'd been pacing and frowning a lot. When he cursed loudly after breaking a fragile ornament, she put down the garland she'd been untangling and stared at him. "What's wrong?"

With a sigh, Jason crossed the room and joined her on the couch. He flashed her an apologetic smile. "I'm sorry for the bellowing, hon. Guess I'm just worried."

She reached out and stroked the rigid line of his jaw. "So I've surmised. Come on, what's troubling you? Spill it out."

He sighed. "It's the Galveston store."

They'd run into some really frustrating construction snags on the new store, such as walls that leaked water and wiring the electrician had assured them was archaic. "Oh, no. Don't tell me the bathroom has sprung another leak?"

He laughed. "I only wish it was that simple. Actually, I've gotten into a real bind."

"Oh?"

His fingers dug into a throw pillow. "Do you remember when I told you that I asked for an increase in financing from my banker due to the cost overruns on the new store?"

"Sure. You were sweating the increase for a while, but Sam Whittaker approved it, right?"

"Yes, he did, but it seems there was a major oversight."

"There was?"

He sighed. "As I've told you before, I'm planning to fill half the Galveston store with the new Home Fires collection of sportswear from Henry Lamont."

She smiled. "I've seen some of their ensembles in magazine ads, and I'm really impressed."

He nodded. "Anyway, Lamont agreed to let me become the exclusive distributor in the Houston-Galveston region, but I had to buy into the line really big in order to establish exclusivity."

"That makes sense. So what's the problem?"

He flung his hands outward in exasperation. "The problem is, the entire cost of the new line was left out of the loan-increase request by mistake."

"Oh, Jason! How did that happen?"

He shook his head in bewilderment. "That's just it. I don't know. I guess some communication glitch between myself and my controller. Ed Simpson swears I never sent him the figures for the new line, and I distinctly remember doing so."

She frowned. "How bad is it?"

"It's a six-figure disaster. Now Ed and I aren't on speaking terms and Sam Whittaker is balking at the overrun. If I can't convince Sam to go out a little further on a limb for me, then I'll face opening the new store half-empty, if at all. Lamont is ready to ship right now, but if I can't get the capital rolling . . ."

Nickie stared at him worriedly. "You really did overextend on this venture, didn't you, Jason? I mean, I remember working with Sam Whittaker before, and he's never denied you an increase."

He drew a heavy breath. "Nickie, times have changed. You of all people should know that it's a tight-money climate right now. I know that the new store will go over big and I'll have no trouble repaying the loan, but I just have to get through this hitch first."

She laid her hand on his. "Would you like me to speak to Sam?"

"Lord, I hate to ask that." He smiled slowly. "But you were so good at such negotiations before, weren't you?"

She nodded. "I could contact the manufacturer and other outlets, and see if I can't gather some figure on the success of the line elsewhere to present to Sam."

"Gee, that would be fantastic." Quickly he added, "But it's too much to ask."

"No, it's not," she answered. "Something has to be done, and if your controller isn't even speaking to you..." She shrugged. "Anyway, I want to see the new store succeed, too."

He grinned. "You're too good to be true." He kissed her quickly. "Sure you don't mind talking to Sam?"

She shook her head. "No problem."

"Great. Thanks, babe." He looked greatly relieved as he stood and walked over to start dismantling the tree.

Yet Nickie felt troubled as she moved to the fireplace and began gathering up the Christmas cards Jason had placed there. In truth, she was happy to help him, but she didn't completely trust his motives. He'd reeled her into helping him with the new store a lot more than she had ever intended. He'd also made it clear that he'd missed working with her, and she couldn't help but wonder how much that lack might have contributed to his motives in wanting her back.

One of the Christmas cards slipped to the floor, and she leaned over to pick it up. The card lay open, and when she glanced at the handwritten message, she felt as if ice water had just been thrown in her face. She stared at the writing, unable to believe her eyes.

"Nickie, what is it?"

She glanced sharply at Jason and held up the card with a trembling hand. "'Great seeing you again. Love, Tracy'?" she quoted furiously.

He turned white as chalk, gulping as he stared at the card. "Oh, that."

"That?" she cried, waving the card at him. "Since when have you been seeing Tracy Wright again?"

"Seeing her?" he repeated in a stunned voice. "I haven't been seeing her at all."

"Then how the hell do you explain this card?" she demanded.

He drew a hand distraughtly through his hair, and the guilt in his expression was obvious. "Nickie, that message is just a reference to the fact that I ran across Tracy at a Christmas party."

"A Christmas party? What party?"

"At the agency where Tracy works."

"You never told me about any party," she accused.

He glanced away miserably. "You had an important audit that afternoon, so I took Stephanie."

"You took Stephanie?" she repeated in a barely audible hiss.

He gestured entreatingly. "Nickie I swear it was only business. I have to maintain my ties with the Zachery Agency. I use them a lot."

"Do you use Tracy a lot?"

His eyes gleamed with hurt. "Nickie, that's not fair!"

"Not fair?" She hurled the card at him and blinked rapidly. "I find an intimate little message from that home wrecker on your fireplace mantel, and all of a sudden *I'm* not being fair?"

He threw up his hands in despair and began to pace. "This is exactly why I didn't tell you. I knew you would react this way."

"You knew, or you didn't want your fun spoiled!" she accused. "Tell me, did you have fun with Tracy at your little party?"

He turned, his eyes bright with anger as he advanced on her. "All right, damn it, if you have to know, Tracy tried flirting with me—and with every other man there. I ignored her, Nickie. It meant nothing to me."

"Then why did you keep her damned card?" she shouted.

"Should I have cared enough to burn it?" he shouted back.

They glared at each other. Nickie was appalled to feel sobs welling up in her chest. She grabbed her purse from the coffee table and made a dash for the door. "I'm going home."

Jason hurried after her and grabbed her arm. His desperate eyes beseeched her. "Nickie, no. Please, no. The party meant nothing. Seeing Tracy meant nothing. Hell, I doubt I said two words to her the whole time. You can ask Stephanie. I swear I'm telling you the truth."

She stared at him, fighting tears and her own mixed feelings. "You didn't even tell me you went, or that you saw her there."

"I know. I was wrong, and I'm sorry." With a groan, he caught her close. "Nickie, Tracy is history. I never use her anymore."

"Never?" she repeated dubiously.

"Never. I promise."

"But the card—"

He caught her face in his hands. "The truth is, I didn't even give the card a thought after I received it. I just put it on the mantel with the others." He stared intently into her eyes. "Darling, if I'd done something I was ashamed of, don't you think I would have hidden the card, or destroyed it?"

"Well, I suppose . . ."

"Hon, you're going to have to trust me a little." When she didn't respond, he added reproachfully, "Nickie? If you want to, we can call Stephanie right now."

Nickie released a heavy breath. "That won't be necessary," she muttered petulantly. In truth, she doubted Stephanie would say anything against Jason.

"Then you'll try to trust me?" Teasingly, he added, "After all, I didn't complain one bit that you spent that whole afternoon with two men down at the IRS."

Her mouth fell open. "You didn't complain? You chase off any man who comes within forty feet of me!"

He grinned and held up a hand. "Okay, so trust is a two-way street. Won't you at least try to believe in me?"

She was silent.

"Nickie?"

"Okay," she conceded grudgingly.

With a deep sigh, he pulled her close and kissed her. "Move back in with me, darling?" he asked urgently.

Despite the fragile peace they'd achieved, moving back in with Jason was the last thing Nickie intended to do right now. She faced him and said firmly, "Jason, you're going to have to give me enough space until I can be really sure—I mean, about us."

He released her with a defeated sigh. "Okay, then." He began working on the tree again.

She returned to gathering up the Christmas cards. "What do you want me to do with these?" she asked awkwardly.

He shrugged. "Throw them away."

"Are you sure?" When his only response was a glower, she added, "I mean, I noticed there was one there from your mother."

He smiled. "I'd like to keep that one."

Nickie set aside the card from Jason's mother, then dumped the other cards—including Tracy's—into the trash. She wished she could dispose of her doubts as easily.

Over the past weeks, she'd worried whether her husband was being completely honest with her. Jason's snide comment to Stephanie. Tracy's sending Jason the Christmas card. Jason's taking Stephanie to the party. By themselves, these gestures might mean nothing. Collectively, they could indicate a pattern. Oh, Lord, had she made a terrible mistake in letting him back into her life?

STANDING ACROSS FROM HER, Jason could feel Nickie's terrible doubts hanging in the air between them, and he felt helpless to rectify things. Damn that card from Tracy. He really hadn't given Tracy's presence at the party—or her subsequent Christmas card—any thought. Now that particular oversight could potentially wreck his reconciliation with his wife.

And he'd asked for Nickie's help with the new store, only minutes before she'd found that innocent yet damning card! In truth, Jason was in a real financial bind with the Galveston store, and he had sincerely appreciated Nickie's offer of help. But now, what was she bound to think? Perhaps just what she'd thought before: that he was a cheat, that he was only using her. Nothing could be further from the truth, but how could he make her believe that?

Was he about to fail at his business *and* his marriage?

THE NEXT DAY, Jason sent Nickie flowers. She stared at the two dozen red roses and wondered why he felt so guilty.

12

ON A SUNNY MORNING in late January, Jason and Nickie drove to the new store in Galveston. Nickie was tired, as she often was these days. She and Jason had managed to maintain a fragile rapport since that disturbing night when Nickie had found Tracy Wright's Christmas card. In truth, Nickie's doubts were far from erased, and she had mixed feelings about the fact that she was still sleeping with him. As she had often mused, her inability to resist Jason was as predictable as the tide rolling in each night.

The fact that they were both frantically busy these days didn't help matters at all. The opening of the Galveston store was only two weeks away now, and sometimes they both feared they'd never make it. Most critical, the additional financing for the new sportswear line still hadn't been approved, although Nickie had made some headway. Furthermore, these efforts took her away from her duties at work, and sometimes she felt pulled in a thousand directions at once.

"You all right, hon?" Jason asked as he turned the car toward the Strand.

She smiled at him weakly. "I'm a little tired."

He frowned. "Hope you're not coming down with that awful flu that's making the rounds at all my stores."

Nickie grimaced. "Actually, Jason, I think I'm kind of running on empty, what with tax time upon us and helping you with the store."

He nodded. "You've been a saint. Speaking of which, has there been any word from Sam Whittaker?"

She shook her head. "No, but he has promised us a final decision as soon as I gather all the figures on the new line."

He gripped the steering wheel tightly. "We'll just have to keep our fingers crossed. Otherwise, the store is going to have a decidedly empty look when it opens—if it does at all."

"Have you considered your options if Sam turns us down?"

He frowned. "I could probably cover most of the cost of the inventory myself, but I'd pretty much have to liquidate everything I own."

She whistled. "Oh, Jason, let's not even think about that yet. At least we've managed to straighten out most of the construction snags, and get the wiring and plumbing up to code."

He waved a hand. "Yes, but now I'm going to have to attend a meeting of one of the local historical societies next week."

"You're what?" Nickie asked.

He tossed her a rueful glance. "Some local eccentric has been raising cane with them about the changes we made to the original facade."

"You mean like replacing those rotted-out doors?" she asked incredulously.

"Yes."

"Good grief."

"I know. This really is a nuisance, since everything we've done has been within the local codes, and the building isn't registered as a historical landmark. But I do need to talk to a few people and smooth over some ruffled feathers. In a community this small, public relations can be critical."

She nodded. "I'm sure you'll do just fine with the locals—they're happy for the jobs. And your plan to use high-school honor students instead of professional models for the opening-day fashion show is a real stroke of genius."

"Community involvement is very important," he agreed.

They fell into a comfortable silence, and Nickie closed her eyes. She didn't realize she had fallen asleep until she felt Jason gently shaking her arm.

They were parked not far from the store, and he was staring at her worriedly. "Perhaps I should take you back to the beach house for a nap."

"No, I'm fine, honestly," she insisted with a yawn. "And I really want to see what progress the workmen have made."

He looked unconvinced. "Sure you're okay?"

She grinned at him crookedly. "You just aren't giving me much opportunity for rest at night."

He chuckled. "Sometimes I forget that not everyone can get by on five hours' sleep, like me." He leaned over and kissed her quickly. "Don't worry, hon. Tonight, I'll let you sleep 'round the clock. We'll just go to bed nice and early to get the—um—preliminaries out of the way."

"Preliminaries," she repeated ruefully. "Now I sound like the first heat in a boxing match."

He stroked her cheek and grinned. "Honey, you're the whole ten rounds."

They laughed as he helped her out of the car. They walked the half block to his store in the brisk, bracing air. As the chill wind sluiced around Nickie's legs, she was glad she'd worn a heavy denim jumpsuit, a knit turtleneck and a thick jacket. Still, she shivered, and Jason wrapped an arm around her.

Outside the glass storefront, they paused, and Jason pointed to the newly etched sign, Stellar Attractions. "What do you think?"

"I think it looks great," she said with forced brightness.

Inside, hammers banged and drills buzzed as craftsmen worked on display cases, and the odor of paint and sawdust filled the air. Nickie usually found such smells pleasant, but today she had to swallow hard and steady herself, since the odors were hitting her all wrong. She tried to distract herself by gazing about at the shop, noting the progress the workmen had made and studying the just-arrived chrome racks filled with spring dresses. For now, the racks were covered in heavy plastic to protect the garments until construction was completed. Boxes of other new merchandise—cosmetics, jewelry and accessories—were stacked about randomly, to be unpacked and displayed as soon as the shop was ready.

Nickie turned to look at Jason, who was eyeing the scene with a satisfied smile. How he seemed to thrive on this type of hustle and bustle! She wondered with sudden uncertainty if their needs could ever really be balanced. Right now, for instance, he was all hard-charging energy, while she was dragging.

"Well, I see a lot of improvement," she commented as they moved on to the second level.

"So do I," he said.

"Jason, Nickie, good morning," came a cheerful voice. Beatrice Langley emerged from the store's back room. Beatrice had been an assistant manager at Jason's Galleria store when he'd asked her to manage the new store.

"Hi, Beatrice," Jason said. "Think we'll be ready to greet the public in two weeks?"

"We'll give it our best shot. If we can just get the sportswear inventory in by then..."

"I know," Jason said feelingly. He wrapped an arm about Nickie's shoulders and added proudly, "We're working on it."

"Great," Beatrice replied with a cheerful smile. "Now, both of you, come to the back room. I want you to see the flyers we received yesterday from the printers."

Nickie and Jason followed Beatrice to the stockroom at the back of the store. With a frown, Nickie observed that most of the racks in the room were empty; they really didn't have enough money to open the store, she thought worriedly.

On a small table, she spotted stacks of silver flyers, neatly displayed in open boxes. She picked one up and examined it. The ad was elegant, done in high-gloss silver, announcing "Galveston's New Stellar Attractions" in handsome black lettering. The festivities were listed, including the champagne opening on Fat Tuesday, with a coupon for ten percent off any initial purchase at the store.

Nickie glanced at Beatrice. "The printers did a beautiful job."

"They sure did," she replied. "The newspapers have already received their flyers for inclusion in next week's edition, and we'll hire some teenagers to distribute the rest of the handbills around town."

"We'll want to reserve a fair amount of flyers for the day of the opening itself, and hire some people to work the crowds," Jason reminded.

"Of course," Beatrice agreed. "Opening during Mardi Gras means thousands of extra people on the island. The special Mardi Gras collection is bound to be a sellout. You're kind of quiet today, Nickie," Beatrice added. "Sure you're feeling okay?"

Jason wrapped an arm around Nickie's waist and answered for her. "I'm afraid she may be coming down with the flu."

"Oh, no! Don't do that," Beatrice said, touching her arm.

"I think I'm just tired," Nickie explained. "Jason and I have been burning the candle at both ends."

"I believe it—with this man," Beatrice replied.

"Anyway, in case I am coming down with the flu, I'll try not to breathe on either of you," Nickie joked.

The three were laughing over her comment when a slim teenage girl with curly red hair and glasses burst into the room. "Hi, Mr. Stellar, Mrs. Stellar, Mrs. Langley."

They all turned toward the newcomer. "Hi, Stacy," Jason said. "What brings you here today?"

The teenager lit up with excitement. "Mrs. Langley phoned to tell me my dress for the fashion show is in."

"It sure is," Beatrice said, going over to a rack in the corner and grabbing a green silk cocktail dress. "Here you are, young lady."

Stacy's eyes widened. "Wow! It's awesome!"

"Go and try it on," Beatrice directed, "so we can see if it will need any alterations before the fashion show."

"Sure, Mrs. Langley!" Grabbing the dress, Stacy dashed off.

A few moments later, Stacy floated out of the rest room in her dress, looking as beautiful as a girl about to leave for the prom.

"It's a perfect fit!" she announced, twirling about. "Can I really keep the dress, Mr. Stellar?"

"You sure can," he informed her proudly.

"Neat!"

"Now, don't forget about rehearsal for the fashion show next Saturday—and remind your friends," Beatrice told the girl.

"I sure will, Mrs. Langley." She whirled around to face Jason. "Can I take the dress home until then, Mr. Stellar? Just to show my mom and my girlfriends?"

"Of course," Jason said.

"Cool!"

Nickie shook her head as she watched Stacy skip off to the bathroom to change again. "It must be great to have that much energy," she told the others.

Jason gave her a quick hug. "You'll be fine, hon, as soon as you get some rest."

The foreman of the construction crew came in and called Jason away to look at the display cases.

Beatrice and Stacy talked for a few minutes before Stacy left.

When Nickie swayed slightly on her feet, Beatrice turned to Nickie. "Are you all right?" she asked. "You look awfully pale, honey." Beatrice pressed her palm to Nickie's forehead. "You don't feel feverish, but—"

"What's going on here?" Jason demanded anxiously.

"I'm afraid your wife may be ill," Beatrice informed Jason, ignoring Nickie's protesting look.

"That does it. It's straight back to the beach house and to bed for you," Jason announced, already grabbing their coats.

Amid Nickie's protests, Jason helped her into her jacket, then donned his own coat and ushered her out of the shop. Out on the street, the frigid air hit her in a blast, and she began to shiver, despite her heavy garb.

"Damn it," Jason said, taking off his jacket and throwing it across her shoulders. "Why didn't you tell me you were feeling so badly?"

"Jason, your coat—you mustn't—"

"Don't worry about me—let's just get you to the car."

Nickie was too miserable to argue as they hurried to the car. The instant they were inside, Jason started the car and turned on the heat, full force. The warmth was very lulling, and Nickie found herself nodding off to sleep again as they drove back to the beach house. It seemed only moments later when she felt Jason's hand on her shoulder. She looked up to see him standing next to her and the car door open.

"Come on, honey, let's get you upstairs," he said.

He wanted to carry her, but when she refused, he didn't argue, no doubt giving in for the sake of expediency. Still, by the time they were inside the door, her teeth were chattering.

"Time to get you to bed," he said grimly, tugging both jackets from her shoulders. "Why don't you just hop in and I'll bring you some soup?"

She nodded and left the room. In the bedroom, she paused only to remove her clothing, then crawled between the sheets.

Jason came in with the instant soup he'd made, but she was too exhausted to eat. Determined to get her warm he got under the covers with his jeans still on, pulling her next to him.

She sighed contentedly and curled her arms around his neck as the delicious heat of his body seeped into hers.

He kissed her forehead and murmured, "If you aren't better by tomorrow, we'll take you to a doctor."

Nickie shivered and nestled herself closer to his warmth. His mention of a doctor made her frown as she

confronted the truth. Her period was late, and she had
been feeling queasy today....

During her previous pregnancy, she'd had no morning sickness at all. Her doctor had told her to count her
blessings; that she was likely one of those women not
prone to that unpleasant symptom.

Still, she *was* late, and Christmas Eve had been the
most fertile period of her cycle.

Could it be that Jason had given her much more for
Christmas than a diamond bracelet and a teddy bear?

13

NICKIE'S CASE OF FLU indeed turned out to be the classic "nine-month virus."

"This is exactly what happens to healthy young women who indulge in sexual relations without benefit of contraception," her doctor pronounced, that momentous morning in early February.

She felt a sudden joy, a fierce happiness that she'd been granted this second chance to have the child she'd wanted for so long. Yet there was also fear—fear that she and Jason might still not make it together, that the timing of this pregnancy could prove disastrous and that—heaven forbid!—she might have to endure again the agony of losing a child.

"You're sure?" she asked the doctor at last.

Dr. Phillips nodded. "We'll have the lab confirm it, of course, but the physical changes I noted seemed unmistakable." He studied her face closely. "You look perturbed, Nickie. Aren't you happy about the pregnancy?"

"Oh, I am," she answered quickly. "It's just that—I'm so scared I could lose the baby again."

He leaned toward her, lacing his fingers together. "I've explained to you several times before that what happened to you during your first pregnancy was a fluke. A certain small percentage of all pregnancies end in spontaneous abortion—and usually, it's a case of a defective embryo, as the lab confirmed in your case. There's no reason to assume this pregnancy will end up the same way."

"But—this pregnancy could be even worse. For instance, I've already had a lot of morning sickness, and I didn't the last time."

Dr. Phillips chuckled. "Actually, Nickie, I see your nausea as a good sign. Often, in the case of a woman who spontaneously aborts, there's been no history of morning sickness during the pregnancy. This is not to say that the absence of morning sickness is any cause for alarm. But again, I feel we can see the presence of nausea as a positive sign in your case."

"I see," Nickie murmured, reassured.

"What about your husband?" Dr. Phillips went on. "You mentioned at your last examination that the two of you had separated." He paused to smile. "Obviously, you must have gotten back together—at least, on some level."

Nickie laughed. "Obviously, we did." More seriously, she continued, "Actually, what I agreed to last fall was a trial reconciliation—but in no time, it seemed, we were back together pretty much as man and wife. And now— Well, to tell you the truth, I'm not sure our marriage is ready for this kind of test."

He frowned thoughtfully. "Have you thought of how losing your baby last year may have precipitated the breakup with Jason?" He picked up a small, brass-framed portrait of his own wife and children, then smiled fondly as he set it back down. "You know, I can't think of anything that would place more stress on a marriage than losing a child."

"That's what Jason said, too," Nickie answered. "So you're saying pretty much what he has—that this baby could cement our relationship?"

"I think that for the two of you to have a child right now could be very healing."

Nickie nodded, but her expression remained troubled. She bit her lip as new anxieties drifted in. "What about my job?"

"I see no reason for you to quit, although it's very important that you not overdo—at anything. You'll probably find that you'll need more rest throughout your pregnancy—and particularly, more sleep during these early months."

"I'll speak with my supervisor at once."

They discussed a few other subjects, such as diet and sex relations, then Nickie thanked her doctor and left. She was immersed in thought as she left the clinic and drove toward Jason's office. While she hadn't told Jason that she would be seeing her doctor today, the two of them did have a date for lunch, and she had some quick thinking to do regarding her news.

Actually, she had a wealth of news for him today. Right before she'd left her office, Sam Whittaker had phoned her, approving Jason's increase in financing. Jason would be overjoyed to hear about this, since he'd already been compelled to sell off a good portion of his stock portfolio to begin shipment of the new Lamont line. Now, he wouldn't have to face liquidating all his personal assets.

When she told Jason about the baby, he'd be as thrilled as she was. But she also knew that he'd try to use her pregnancy to solidify their relationship, that he'd insist that they move back in together, be a family.

Her being pregnant did change things. Whether or not she and Jason stayed together as husband and wife, they would always be the mother and father of this child.

If she carried the child to term. Despite Dr. Phillips's reassurances to the contrary, she still very much feared that her and Jason's marital problems before may have contributed to her miscarriage—and there was no way she would risk watching history repeat itself.

She remembered when she'd become pregnant last year. When she'd told Jason, he'd become consumed with ambition, wanting to expand his business quickly and drastically and make everything perfect before the baby arrived. He'd begun traveling too much, drinking too much, and was constantly around other, beautiful women—

Nickie knew she could never endure such emotional stress again. Yet already, she could spot signs of troubles popping up in their relationship again, such as Jason's frantic, nonstop activity readying the new store. Now, when she told him about the baby, could she trust him to react in a way that would be more responsive to her needs, or would he again indulge in the type of excessive, destructive behavior that had torn them apart before?

Nickie had other troubles on her mind, as well.

This Sunday, her mother was hosting a family reunion to honor the christening of Meredith's baby, and Nickie's father and his wife would be coming from California. Nickie dreaded seeing her dad again, and she still felt miffed and puzzled as to why her mother had invited them both.

Of course, Jason had also been invited, and if she told him about the baby before Sunday, he'd be certain to make an announcement in front of everyone. Then her entire family would surely think—

Oh, Lord, she couldn't cope with all of this right now. When had everything become so complicated?

WHEN NICKIE WALKED into Jason's office, she was shocked to see a red-eyed, puffy-faced Stephanie loading her personal effects into a box. "Stephanie—are you all right?"

The girl appeared acutely embarrassed, avoiding Nickie's gaze. "Oh, hello, Mrs. Stellar. Shall I tell your husband you're here?"

"Yes, but— What's wrong?"

Stephanie's chin came up. "As I'm sure you can see, I'm leaving."

"But—why?"

"I think you'd better ask Mr. Stellar about that." She leaned over and flipped on the intercom. "Mr. Stellar, your wife is here." After his muffled reply drifted out, she added, "Yes, I'll send her right in."

Puzzled, Nickie walked into Jason's office. He stood by the windows with his back to her. There was tension in every line of his tall, lithe body.

She shut the door gently. "Jason?"

He turned to her with a strained smile. "Hi, hon." He strode to her side and kissed her cheek. "How are you doing?"

"Oh, I'm fine."

"Do you have news for me?"

For a moment, Nickie was taken aback. "News about what?"

"Sam Whittaker?"

"Oh, right." She smiled tightly. "He called earlier this morning, approving your increase."

Jason's face lit up. "Great!" He swung her around and kissed her soundly. "I knew you'd pull it off! Babe, you're fantastic!"

Yet Nickie was frowning as he set her on her feet. "Jason, what's going on with Stephanie?"

He raked a hand through his hair. "Oh, that."

"Yes, that."

"I'm afraid she quit."

"Quit? Why?"

He sighed miserably. "If you must know, she and I had—well, something of a confrontation."

Nickie felt the color drain from her face. "A confrontation? Over what?"

Looking uncharacteristically self-conscious, Jason began to pace. "Evidently she's been in love with me for some time, and she must have learned something of our marital problems from her coworkers. Anyway, earlier this morning, she demanded to know whether you and I are really getting back together again. When I told her we definitely *are* back together, she resigned on the spot."

"Good Lord!" Nickie gasped. "Jason, how could you let her think—"

He stared at her incredulously. "Nickie, I never came on to Stephanie—in any way!"

She bit her lip. "Perhaps you didn't, but neither did you tell her about the reconciliation."

"And I explained to you why I felt my marital status was none of her business," he replied heatedly.

"Still, you must have encouraged her in some way."

His hand sliced the air. "Encouraged her? How can you say that?"

"You took her to the Christmas party," she accused.

He appeared stunned. "Nickie, that was business."

"Was it?" She shrugged fatalistically. "Women always fall for you."

"And that's my fault?"

"I don't know, Jason. I just don't know."

Nickie walked over to the windows and stood staring out at the skyline. Panic threatened to consume her.

What had she done? She had loved Jason again, conceived his child. But were they destined to repeat the same mistakes?

Jason came up behind her and placed his hands on her shoulders. "Nickie, why can't you trust me? You have to know that you're the only woman for me."

Nickie couldn't answer, suddenly choked by tears.

"Look, let's get out of here and go have lunch." He leaned over and kissed her neck, and she shivered. "Then tonight, I'm going to spend a lot of time proving just how much you mean to me."

Nickie stiffened at his words. She turned to him, her expression torn. "Jason—about tonight. Look, I'm way behind at work. I just think it would be better if we don't spend the next few nights together."

"Damn it, Nickie, why are you letting this come between us?" he demanded furiously.

"I'm just tired, Jason. Really tired." There, at last, she had spoken the truth.

He sighed. "You do look wiped out, hon, and you haven't been quite yourself ever since you had that virus a couple of weeks ago. But why do I still feel as if I'm losing you?"

She touched his arm reassuringly. "You're not losing me. I just need some space. Just for a few days."

He frowned at her for a moment, then nodded. "Okay. On one condition—you're still coming with me to Galveston this weekend."

"Sure, Jason."

"You know next Tuesday is the opening. I can't get through it without you. Hell, if it hadn't been for you, we might not even be opening the store."

"Right," she said with a strained smile. "You really need me for the opening, don't you?"

"Nickie, what is it?"

"It's nothing," she lied.

He studied her suspiciously. "Promise me you won't try to weasel out of going to Galveston?"

"Promise." Biting her lip, she added, "But we mustn't forget that we have to come back on Sunday for the christening of Meredith's baby, and the family gathering Mom is planning."

Suddenly, Jason looked relieved. "Aha!" he said, waving a finger. "So that's it. You're still worried about seeing your dad and his wife?"

"I'm sure it will all be awkward," she admitted.

"But you want to attend?"

"Of course. We can't miss the baby's christening."

He nodded. "How are Meredith and the baby doing?"

"Just great. Mere's very excited about Sunday."

"Then we'll be sure to come back." Extending his arm to her, he added, "Ready for lunch? After all, we have some celebrating to do."

Nickie smiled ruefully. He was referring to their success with the banker, of course—not to the baby. "Sure."

As they walked through the outer office, Stephanie was just finishing up her packing. They paused before the girl's desk, and Stephanie tossed Jason an anguished look. Nickie's heart went out to the girl. She realized that she had every right to feel angry and jealous toward Stephanie, yet instead she commiserated totally. After all, she'd been in Stephanie's shoes before—and might well be there again. She knew exactly what it felt like to love Jason Stellar hopelessly, and to fear that that love was doomed.

Jason smiled stiffly at the young woman. "Stephanie, I wish you'd reconsider. You've been a very good secretary."

"I'm sorry, sir. I just can't," she said tightly.

"Well . . . good luck to you, then."

She nodded, glancing away. "Just have my final check sent to my home address."

"Sure. I'll have it sent there, along with a letter of recommendation."

"Thanks."

"Need some help with the box?"

"No, thank you. You two go on—enjoy your lunch."

Stephanie's last words came out half strangled. Jason stared at the girl in bewilderment for a moment, then took Nickie's arm and firmly escorted her out of the office. As they walked silently toward the elevator, Nickie felt an emptiness in the pit of her stomach that she knew food could never fill.

Predictably, her lunch with Jason was awkward, their conversation strained.

She didn't tell him about the baby.

14

JASON AND NICKIE didn't see each other for the remainder of the week. Nickie knew that he was busy with the Galveston opening, and she was just as involved in her work. She did talk with her supervisor about lightening up her duties now that she was pregnant, and he readily agreed. He also praised her work and let her know that her future with the firm was secure. It made Nickie feel good to know that she'd be able to provide for her child, whether or not she and Jason were together.

After speaking with her boss, Nickie felt guilty that she still hadn't told Jason about her pregnancy, but she promised herself that she would this weekend.

The two of them did have a brief, strained conversation on Thursday, when Jason informed Nickie that he would be driving down to Galveston on Friday afternoon and asked her to accompany him. Nickie couldn't get away that soon, and offered instead to meet him there on Saturday.

That day dawned cold but sunny. Nickie had agreed to meet Jason at the beach house at two. When she pulled into the carport at one forty-five, she saw that his Mercedes was already parked there. She hurried up the outside steps, turning up her collar against the chill wind.

When she swept into the living room, the heat of a wood fire curled out to warm her. Jason was across the room, pacing and talking on the phone, a preoccupied frown marring his perfect features.

Upon spotting her, he smiled and waved, then said into the phone, "Hey, Frank, my wife's here, can I call you back later?" A moment later, he hung up and hurried over to greet her.

"Hi, hon," he said, pulling her into his arms and kissing her.

She hugged him back. "Hi, Jason."

"Here, let me help you with your coat."

"Thanks." After he took her coat, she walked across the room to warm her hands in front of the fire. As he joined her there, picking up a poker and soberly stabbing at the logs, she remarked, "You look tense."

He nodded, setting down the poker. "To be honest, Nickie, I've had a really frustrating day. I was just talking with the shipping dock at my Galleria store in Houston. Some of the dresses for the fashion show still haven't come in, and the shipment may be lost."

"Oh, no! I'm sorry, Jason. It's been one stumbling block after another with the new store, hasn't it?"

He sighed. "Unfortunately, this type of thing seems to be par for the course."

"It was good of you to take the time to break away and come meet me," she said with a smile.

He wrapped an arm about her waist and grinned. "I wouldn't have missed it for the world. Everything else may be unraveling, but you're my sanity, as always."

Even though he spoke lightly, Nickie could sense the anxiety behind his words and his smile. "What else has gone wrong?" she asked.

Suddenly he looked uneasy, avoiding her gaze. "Oh, just a number of last-minute complications," he said vaguely. "We'll get everything resolved, I'm sure." Standing back slightly, he gave her the once-over, taking in her jeans and sweater, her wind-mussed hair and cold-flushed features. "So, how are things with you?"

She stifled a yawn. "Guess I'm feeling harried these days, like you."

He pulled her close and leaned over to nibble at the curve of her jaw. "Why don't we go take a little nap, catch up on our rest?"

Even though Nickie's pulse quickened at his suggestion, she managed to laugh and teased back, "Well, with you, the notion of going to bed *to rest* is certainly ludicrous. Besides, I thought you said you were busy today, with all your last-minute complications."

"I'm never too busy for you," he said eagerly.

Nickie managed to squirm out of his grasp. "I guess I'm not in the mood for a quick tumble right now," she replied—much more irritably than she had intended.

He appeared stunned, the color draining from his face. "A quick tumble? Since when have you characterized our love life that way?"

She met his gaze contritely. "Sorry, Jason, I didn't mean it the way it sounded. It's just—poor timing."

He threw a hand wide in exasperation. "Nickie, what is it with you? Lately, you haven't been in the mood, period. You've gone from climbing all over me to—" Before he could finish, the phone rang. Muttering an oath, he strode off to answer it.

"Yeah—I'll be right there." He sat down the receiver and turned back to her, his expression grim. "That was the Strand store. I've got to get over there immediately."

"Want me to come? I'd love to see the store now that everything's almost ready."

He shook his head, and again he avoided her eyes. "Look, Nickie, you really do look tired. Why don't you go ahead and have a nap? I'll pick you up later and take you to see the store."

"Sure," she said with a shrug.

AFTER JASON LEFT, Nickie decided she did need a nap. She felt badly that she hadn't told Jason about the baby as soon as she'd arrived. But they'd both been so tense just now—almost like strangers. She couldn't just spill out her news when they were like that.

Her mind was preoccupied with other worries, too—work, the opening of the Strand store, and especially, tomorrow's reunion and her certain meeting with her father and his second wife.

Finally Nickie drifted off into a fitful slumber, but it seemed that she had no sooner shut her eyes than she was rudely awakened by the phone.

"Hello?" she managed sleepily.

"Is this Nickie?" the male caller asked.

"Yes."

"Nickie, this is Claude White, manager of the Galleria store. Is Jason there?"

"No, he's down at the Strand store," Nickie replied. "Do you need the number?"

"No, thank you. Actually, I've been trying to get through to the store for about an hour now, but the line is busy. And unfortunately, I can't stay here much longer. I was wondering— Could you get a message to Jason?"

"Of course."

"Please tell him that we have managed to locate the rest of the dresses for the fashion show. The shipment was sent to the southwest Houston store by mistake. And please let him know that I'm going to pick up the shipment myself and drive it down to the Galveston store immediately."

"That's very kind of you, Claude. Jason will be thrilled to learn that you've found the dresses. And I'll be sure to give him the message."

After they hung up, Nickie tried the number of the Strand store, only to find that the line was still busy. Feeling restless, she decided to drive into town to deliver the message to Jason in person.

She dressed and grabbed her coat and purse. As she stepped out on the stoop, she noted that the day had turned cold and blue. A norther appeared to be blowing in, and the waves looked fierce and angry as they pounded against the shoreline.

Nickie shivered as she hurried down the steps and got into her car. The drive into town took about ten minutes, and she felt much better as the warmth of the heater washed over her. She parked close to Jason's store and held her coat tightly about her as she hurried along the windswept sidewalk.

Outside the store, she paused briefly, eyeing with appreciation the Mardi Gras window display—masked mannequins in glittery ball gowns were perched amid treasure chests spilling out their booty. Black fisherman's nets, dripping with gold doubloons, were looped from the ceiling to complete the nautical fantasy.

Nickie swept inside, welcoming the warmth pumped out by the new central-heating system. The sound system was working, too, she noted, as light rock spilled out from the overhead speakers. A couple of workmen were busy tacking down carpet, but otherwise the store looked almost ready—perfumes, jewelry and cosmetics filled the glass display cases and countertops at the front of the store, while the newly arrived Lamont sportswear collection hung from shiny chrome racks on the second level beyond. Warm track lighting washed the merchandise

with a soft glow. Everywhere was the smell of new-
ness—crisp fabrics, fresh paint, new carpet.

Moving to the center of the store, Nickie spotted Beatrice Langley, who stood behind a counter talking on the
telephone, a stack of invoices in front of her. She was
obviously trying to deal with some last-minute delivery
problems. No wonder the phone had been busy for so
long, Nickie thought. She waved at Beatrice, who waved
in response as Nickie went on toward the back room,
looking for Jason.

As soon as Nickie stepped inside, she froze, horrified,
as the nauseating smell of Tracy Wright's custom-mixed
perfume wafted over her. It was a smell she would never
forget—the very smell that had been on Jason's shirt the
night they had lost their child.

For a moment, her senses recoiled, and she desperately hoped she'd made a mistake. But soon her eyes
confirmed what her nose already knew: In the middle of
the room stood Jason with three gorgeous, scantily clad
models—and one of them was Tracy! Indeed, Tracy was
wearing only a short black slip, her gorgeous long legs
totally revealed. Jason was kneeling on the floor at her
feet, pulling a black cocktail dress from a box. As Nickie
watched, he stood, holding the straps of the dress against
Tracy's bare shoulders—*touching* her. She trembled,
feeling as if he had just plunged a knife into her heart.
How could he do this to her, after declaring that he never
used Tracy?

Tracy spotted Nickie before Jason did. She flashed
Nickie a smile—a sultry, triumphant smile. Then Jason
followed Tracy's gaze and saw his wife. He dropped the
dress and started toward her. "Nickie—"

But she was already turning and rushing out the door.
She reeled with hurt and bitter memories as she fled the

shop. It all came back to her—Jason lying to her, Jason being with other women, and all the horrors of the night she'd lost her child.

What a fool she'd been! She'd been caught up in the magic of loving Jason—of being seduced by him—when he really hadn't changed at all. She remembered the Christmas card Tracy had sent him— They might have been having an affair all along! And even if they weren't, women would always fall in love with Jason—Stephanie, Tracy or someone equally ravishing. And in some way, he *must* be encouraging them. She'd never be able to trust him. She could see the same vicious cycle starting up all over again, and she just couldn't endure it another time. She had to protect herself. She couldn't, *wouldn't*, lose this child. She had to break away.

Nickie was tearing headlong into the street when steely fingers gripped her arm. She caught a brief, harrowing image of a swiftly passing truck before she was hauled up hard against Jason.

"Are you trying to get yourself killed?" he asked in a strangled tone, his features white.

She was suddenly choked with tears. "Let me go!"

"No. Not until you tell me why you just ran out of the store."

Tears spilled down her cheeks, and her words burst forth in an angry torrent. "You know damned well why! Because you're a liar and a cheat, just like before. Because you'll never be happy with just me. So why don't you just admit it!"

"Nickie, that's not true—or fair."

"True? Fair?" she repeated bitterly. "Who are you to talk about truth and fairness when your word means nothing? Why don't you just go back and finish dressing—or undressing—Tracy!"

"Nickie, damn it, let's go back inside so I can explain—"

"No!"

He gripped her shoulders tightly and continued passionately, "All right, then, we'll talk right here. Getting the store finished in time has been a nightmare. Not only did the shipment of dresses get lost, but three of the girls who were supposed to model for the fashion show just came down with the flu. I've been forced to hire three Houston models, and now I'm trying desperately to throw together outfits for each of them to wear on Tuesday."

"Why did you have to hire Tracy?" she cried furiously. "You promised me you wouldn't!"

"I know I did," he admitted miserably. "But Tracy was one of the few models available."

"Don't you know what I felt when I smelled her perfume again?" she demanded, choking on her sobs. "Everything came back. The miscarriage...all the things we lost."

Jason hauled her shivering body close. "Hon, I know. I'm sorry."

She shoved him away. "Why didn't you tell me?"

He spoke plaintively. "Because I knew it would bring back those painful memories for you. I wanted to spare you that. Darling, please, she means nothing to me. No one means anything to me but you. I need you, Nickie."

"You need me?" she repeated bitterly. A deep heartache and terrible resignation filled her eyes, her voice. "I think just the opposite is true. The new store finally made it, didn't it? You don't need me at all anymore."

"Nickie, how can you say that?"

"I can! I'm sorry, but I just can't take this anymore. Whatever way you put it, you lied to me. I can't trust you, Jason."

"Doesn't it matter at all that I love you?" he cried desperately.

But even as he stood, brokenheartedly calling her name, she turned and ran for her car.

15

AN HOUR LATER, Jason's expression was grim as he strode into the bar of a hotel down the street from his shop. He was the only customer, and he welcomed the solitude. He'd really blown things now.

He'd made a big mistake in not telling Nickie that he was substituting Tracy and the other two models in the fashion show. Yet he'd been truly desperate, on the verge of having to cancel the show. If he had told Nickie about Tracy beforehand, would her reaction really have been any different?

Over the past few weeks, Jason had sensed himself and Nickie drifting apart. He knew part of the problem had been the demands of their careers, and especially, of getting the new store off the ground. Still, Nickie had been pulling away from him ever since she'd found the card from Tracy, and her remoteness had become increasingly apparent after Stephanie had quit earlier this week. That episode—when Jason had been forced to admit to Nickie that Stephanie had fallen in love with him—had prompted him to withhold the information about Tracy and the other models. Nickie had seemed so upset over the incident with Stephanie that he'd feared that if he told her about Tracy, she would have walked out on him.

Hell, that was funny. For as things had turned out, she'd walked out on him, anyway. The girl would never trust him.

"May I get you a drink, sir?"

Jason looked up to see a pretty blond cocktail waitress staring down at him with her order pad in hand. If Nickie were here right now, he mused ruefully, she'd doubtless be jealous of this girl, too, just because she was smiling at him. What was he supposed to do? Live the rest of his life in a glass cage?

Jason was sorely tempted to order himself a stiff Scotch. He wavered for an agonizing moment, then brought himself sharply back to reality. He knew he mustn't let his frustration over his marriage undermine what had been an important personal decision. Certainly his breakup with Nickie last year had precipitated his giving up booze, but sobriety was a life choice he'd made mostly for himself. That choice had worked out well for him personally, even if his marriage was again in chaos. If he took another drink now, he'd only be lashing out at himself, not Nickie.

"Sir?"

He flashed the waitress a thin smile. "Bring me a Perrier, please," he said tightly.

As the girl walked away, Jason sighed and returned to his unhappy thoughts. Was there any way he could get through to Nickie, any way he could reach her? Right now, he just didn't know.

BACK AT HER TOWN HOUSE in Houston, Nickie was also agonizing. Her mind kept drifting back to those awful moments at the Galveston store, when she'd seen Jason with Tracy. She had wanted so badly to believe in him, but he had broken his promise and shaken her fragile trust. Now she couldn't help but wonder again what might have been going on between him and Tracy.

Nickie was still mulling this over when the phone rang. She picked up the receiver with a frown. "Hello?"

"Mrs. Stellar?" came a familiar feminine voice.

"Yes?"

"It's Stephanie Burns. You know, Mr. Stellar's former secretary?"

"Oh, hi. How are you?" Nickie asked stiffly.

Stephanie laughed. "I'm surprised you're even being civil with me. Look, I'm calling to apologize for making such a fool of myself the other day, when I quit."

"You don't have to apologize," Nickie said politely.

"But I do." Stephanie released a heavy breath. "I just wanted you to know that there was never anything going on between Mr. Stellar and me. He never did anything to encourage me. It was all me."

"I see," Nickie murmured rather skeptically.

"Mr. Stellar is just one of those men that women always fall in love with," Stephanie continued wistfully.

"That he is," Nickie agreed.

"I mean, I can't tell you how many women came into the office and made fools of themselves over him," Stephanie continued. "Mr. Stellar always looked so bewildered, as if he had no idea why he affected them that way. And you should have seen the way Tracy Wright was falling all over him at the Christmas party we attended. The poor guy was embarrassed to death."

Suddenly Nickie was suspicious. "Did Jason put you up to this call?"

"Oh, no," Stephanie answered quickly and forcefully. "I haven't even spoken to him since I quit."

"Then how did you get my home phone number?"

"Actually, I still have your address and phone number in one of my notebooks, from when Mr. Stellar sent you flowers."

Nickie nodded. She was silent for a long moment. At last she dared to ask, "So my husband did nothing to encourage Tracy Wright at the Christmas party?"

"Nothing at all. Honestly, Mrs. Stellar, I've never seen him encourage any woman."

"Jason just hired Tracy for a job," Nickie admitted.

Stephanie was quiet a moment. "Then he must have been really desperate, because I remember him telling me several times that it was our policy never to use Tracy Wright."

Nickie sighed. "I really appreciate your calling, Stephanie."

"Sure. And Mrs. Stellar?"

"Yes?"

"You know, Mr. Stellar really is crazy about you. I don't mean to meddle, but I've noticed that things aren't quite right between the two of you, and I really hope you'll give him a chance."

"Thanks, Stephanie."

She hung up, but she couldn't get the conversation out of her head.

THE NEXT MORNING, Nickie awakened feeling depressed and missing Jason terribly. She also feared she had overreacted at the Galveston store yesterday. During the course of the long night, she'd examined her own behavior.

Yes, Jason had been dishonest with her, withholding important information. But how would she have reacted if he had told her about Tracy beforehand? She knew that no matter how good Jason's excuse, she would have reacted to Tracy's presence in a wildly jealous way.

Nickie got ready for church, wondering if Jason would show up for the christening. She tried to analyze her gloomy feelings about the coming day. Of course, she felt happy for her sister and Richard's sake; and she wouldn't miss her tiny nephew's christening for the world. But she also dreaded being around her father and his wife. Nickie had met her several times, and she had to concede that Sandra was a nice enough person. But Sandra's stunning good looks reinforced Nickie's feeling that her dad had wanted a "trophy" wife in his later years; that he'd deserted her mom for superficial reasons.

Nickie arrived at the church early. Stepping into the foyer, she observed that her mother and Steve were already there, as were Meredith, Richard and the guest of honor, tiny Richard, Jr. She was greeted effusively by them. Vivian explained that Mack and his wife were still at the house dressing the children, but that they should be arriving shortly. Both Steve and Meredith asked about Jason, and Nickie replied stiffly that he should be joining them later. To avoid further queries, Nickie asked to hold the baby. She cuddled her precious nephew and kissed his little cheek, thinking of the tiny life growing inside her own body.

Right after Nickie had returned the baby to Meredith, she watched her dad and Sandra enter the church through the double glass doors. She felt a twinge of nervousness. Watching the two cross the foyer together, Nickie had to admit that her father and Sandra made a stunning couple. Malcolm Smith was a handsome, graying man in his mid-fifties; Sandra was around thirty-five, the very image of coiffed blond perfection. Both were impeccably dressed—Malcolm in a superbly cut gray suit and Sandra in a purple silk designer dress and a mink jacket.

The two now joined the others, and Nickie's mother was the first to step forward to greet the newcomers.

"Malcolm, Sandra, we're glad you made it," she said politely, offering her hand to each of them in turn.

"Good to see all of you," Malcolm replied.

Meredith approached with the baby. "Hi, Dad," she said warmly. "Meet your new grandchild."

Malcolm turned to Meredith with a delighted grin. "Meredith, you look wonderful," he said, kissing her on the cheek. "And what a beautiful baby."

"Thanks, Dad."

"May I hold him?"

"Of course." Meredith slipped the baby into her father's arms.

Malcolm beamed with pride as he held the child. He then turned to Nickie, leaning over to kiss her forehead. "Nickie, dear, how are you?"

"I'm fine, Dad," she replied with a stiff smile. "I'm glad you—and Sandra—could make it for the christening."

"We wouldn't have missed it," Malcolm assured her.

"We're so happy to be included," Sandra concurred with a smile, and Nickie nodded to her politely.

"Malcolm, I do hope you and Sandra are planning to join us at the house for lunch after the service," Vivian put in.

"We'd be delighted," Malcolm replied graciously.

"Are you two going to be in town for long?" Steve added, his expression showing much greater constraint.

"Oh, for a few days," Malcolm replied casually. "Long enough to see the sights and have a visit with everyone."

Mack and his family arrived just then, prompting a new wave of hugs and greetings. After all the small talk had been exhausted, the family members adjourned to seat themselves inside the church. Nickie sat with her brother's family, while the rest of the clan sat in front of them, with the exception of Malcolm and Sandra, who sat apart from the others, across the aisle.

Waiting for the service to begin, Nickie mulled over her mother's gracious inclusion of her dad and Sandra in the family gathering. Steve hadn't seemed entirely pleased, but Nickie knew that he was too fine a man to ever say a critical word to Vivian about her invitation. Nickie, however, felt her mother had been much too cordial with her father, considering his betrayal and desertion twelve years ago.

Nickie was much moved by the christening ritual. Her eyes misted as she watched Meredith and Richard walk up the aisle to stand before the minister with their baby. Her heart turned over at the look of quiet joy husband and wife exchanged. Would she and Jason ever know such a moment with their child? she wondered achingly. Or would she be walking up that aisle alone with her baby?

Nickie watched the minister baptize her nephew with holy water, and she joined in with the congregation's laughter at the baby's lusty cry. The infant quieted as soon as he was returned to his mother's arms, and the little family returned to their pew.

Soon the benediction was said and the service ended. Glancing around the crowded church, Nickie noted that Jason still hadn't appeared. She sighed in disappointment.

Nickie's moroseness deepened as she drove to her mother's house. The poignant beauty of the christening service had certainly emphasized what was at stake for her now. She wanted what her brother and sister both had: a loving family. But could she and Jason really make it? She wasn't sure. She did know she could support and raise her child on her own; but did she really want to?

At her mom's, Nickie helped the other women get the food ready out in the kitchen. Jason still hadn't put in an appearance, and Nickie's spirits continued to sag.

A few minutes before luncheon was to be served, Mack passed around glasses of wine and sparkling grape juice, and then Nickie's mother led a toast for everyone out in the living room. Raising her glass proudly, she said, "To our family—and especially, to its newest member." A cheer went up from the group.

As Nickie's mother turned to go back to the kitchen, Nickie watched her dad approach Vivian and touch her on the shoulder. She turned and the two spoke briefly. Vivian smiled and touched Malcolm's arm before taking his glass and returning to the kitchen.

Bemused, Nickie followed her mother into the kitchen. Helping Vivian wash the wineglasses, she remarked, "I've noticed that you and Dad seem to be getting along pretty well."

"I suppose we are," Vivian replied.

"Actually, I was shocked that you even invited him today."

Vivian sighed. "Well, dear, I guess I've arrived at the point where I want to smooth things out in my life. I'm really happy with Steve, and after all these years, I've decided it's time to give up my bitterness over Malcolm."

"I see." But she didn't understand at all.

After a moment, Vivian continued thoughtfully. "If you want to know the truth, Nickie, I think I've come to realize that to some degree, I, too, was responsible for the breakup of Malcolm's and my marriage."

Nickie almost dropped the wineglass she was washing. "Mom! How can you say that? After the way Dad cheated on you—"

"I'll admit that Malcolm always had a roving eye," Vivian cut in. "But I've come to realize that I was partly responsible. You see, I always was irrationally jealous. I never could believe that your father would be satisfied with a wallflower like me. I'm not saying that his cheating was justified. But I have come to feel that in some ways, I drove him away."

Amazed, Nickie asked, "Mom, how did you come to this conclusion?"

Vivian looked at her daughter with a sad, compassionate smile. "Because I see you doing the same thing with Jason."

"What?" Nickie gasped.

"The two of you are apart again, aren't you, dear?" Vivian asked gently.

Nickie nodded. "We had a fight yesterday." Miserably, she confessed, "Mom, I've tried, but I just can't seem to trust him."

Vivian set down her dish towel and touched Nickie's arm. "Honey, I know it's hard. But I think you have to consider the possibility that some of this could be you."

Nickie laughed bitterly. "Actually, that's just what I've been thinking about during the past twenty-four hours." She shook her head and studied her mother with new appreciation. "You've always loved Jason, haven't you?"

"Oh, yes."

"Why?"

Vivian squeezed Nickie's arm and said earnestly, "Because I've always known that he's nothing like your father. Give him a chance, Nickie. Make a leap of faith. Don't make the same mistakes I did."

Nickie mulled over her mother's words as she finished washing the glasses. Vivian's revelations certainly demonstrated to her that things in life were rarely etched out in black-and-white. All these years, she had blamed her father exclusively for the breakup of her parents' marriage, when things couldn't have been quite that simple. Now she had to consider the possibility that she could be following the same destructive path her mother had chosen.

"Make a leap of faith," her mom had said. Trusting Jason would certainly involve a leap of faith, for Nickie could never control or watch his every move. She would have to become willing to let him go a little and trust him around other women. Otherwise her doubts and her possessiveness would destroy everything they had.

As Nickie took a large fruit salad out to the dining room table, she noted that her father and Sandra were seated alone in the living room beyond, both looking ill at ease. Nickie went over to sit beside them. "So you're going to be in town a few days, Dad?" she asked.

Her father glanced fondly at Sandra. "Perhaps as long as a week. Sandra would like to do some sight-seeing while we're here—take in NASA, and perhaps even go down to Galveston for a day or two during Mardi Gras."

"You'll both love Galveston," Nickie said eagerly. "In fact, my husband, Jason, is opening a new store there on Tuesday."

"Vivian mentioned that," Malcolm said. "Tell me, is Jason coming today? We've never had the pleasure of meeting him, you know."

"I know, but—I'm just not sure he can make it today," Nickie said awkwardly.

"Then could Sandra and I take the two of you out to dinner sometime later this week?" Malcolm asked.

"That would be nice," Nickie replied tactfully. "However, if Jason is still too busy, could the three of us go instead?"

"Of course, that would be fine," Malcolm replied.

"We must be sure to make a date before we leave today," Sandra added.

The three of them were still chatting when the doorbell rang. Nickie glanced toward the foyer, then her heart tripped into a frantic rhythm as she watched Jason enter. The sight of him thrilled her so, she almost forgot all her apprehensions. He looked so handsome and so solemn, standing there in his dark blue suit. He was carrying a plush white teddy bear—smaller than Stellar Bear, but still large.

Meredith and Richard immediately showed him the baby, and Jason's features lit up. He kissed Meredith's cheek, handed Richard the teddy bear, and then asked to hold the infant. Still cuddling him, Jason turned toward the living room and saw Nickie. Their gazes locked for a meaningful moment. There was so much emotion in his eyes that Nickie was forced to look away.

Minutes later, he stood before her. She lurched to her feet, her heart pounding, and stared up at him guiltily. Why did he have to look so irresistible, and smell so good, and stare at her with such intensity? She realized she wanted to do nothing more than throw herself into his arms and say, *Oh, darling, you looked so good holding that baby....* Instead, she managed a breathy, "Hi, Jason. I'd like you to meet my father, Malcolm Smith, and his wife, Sandra."

By now, Nickie's father was also standing and extending his hand. "Good to meet you, Jason."

Jason firmly shook the other man's hand. "You, too, sir. And nice to meet you, Sandra."

"Same here," Sandra said with a smile, also shaking Jason's hand.

"I was just telling Nickie that we'd love to take the two of you out to dinner this week," Malcolm continued.

"That's a great idea, but you must let us treat you," Jason replied. "However, for the moment, I really must talk to Nickie. So, if you'll excuse us...?"

"Of course," Malcolm said.

Without further ado, Nickie found herself being dragged off by her husband. His expression was grim as he led her off to the study.

Once they were inside, he shut the door, then turned to face her squarely. Yet his voice trembled as he said, "Nickie, I was wrong not to tell you about Tracy."

She nodded. "I know. But I was wrong to expect you never to be around another beautiful woman."

He stared at her a moment. "Perhaps so. At any rate, I think I have a solution."

Her heart seemed to climb into her throat. "Oh?"

He nodded with determination. "I'm shutting it down. I'm pulling the plug on the Galveston store."

"Are you crazy?"

"Never more sane."

"But you told me you *had* to have that store. I assumed that there was some critical business reason—"

"Yes, there was a critical reason," he said. "You."

Nickie was too flabbergasted to comment.

Jason began to pace, saying, "I'll admit that I'd had my eye on the Galveston rental for some time, and I always felt a store would go over well there. But I made the decision to commit mainly because of you. That's the way we fell in love before—working on my business together. And things were always good for us there, at your beach house in Galveston. I wanted to go back to the beginning and get it right this time. But I also wanted to get you away from the corporate atmosphere, the glitz, all the things you found threatening. That's what made the Galveston location so perfect. It was a way to keep you with me, to throw us together and give us a chance to get reacquainted—"

Laughing, Nickie cut in incredulously, "By starting an entire new store? It would have been a lot cheaper to buy me candy or flowers, or invite me out to dinner, Jason."

Distraught, he stared at her, obviously not the least bit amused by her comments. "Nickie, you were always what kept my feet on the ground. But I always ruined it. You gave me a second chance, but everything fell apart on us again. I thought the store would bring us closer together, but it didn't. Now, I just don't know what else I can do to convince you how much I love you, how much you mean to me—"

"I think you already have," she said. Shaking her head, she added, "I've never had anyone do a store for me before. It's the sweetest thing I've ever heard of. I'll have to say it's 'Stellar' in every way. You must really love me, Jason."

"What do you think I've been trying to convince you of for the last two and a half years?" he asked in frustration.

"Oh, Jason," she said, rushing into his arms. "I'm so sorry. I love you so much—"

Further speech was silenced as his lips roughly took hers. The distance between them dissolved in a moment of joyous healing and reconciliation. Kissing Jason back eagerly, Nickie reflected on the irony of the situation. Here, she had feared that Jason might be using her for business purposes, when it couldn't have been further from the truth. He had even started an entire store just to bring them closer together. She realized with awe that Jason Stellar also had his insecurities, that he was every bit as afraid of losing her as she was of losing him. She also realized that her own doubts and fears about being the right woman for him had surely put him through hell. Now it was time to really make things up to him—

Before she could voice her thoughts, Jason pulled back and said passionately, "Just give us a chance, Nickie. If you don't want the new store, I'll shut it down. I'll sell out the whole damned chain if that's what it takes."

"It won't work Jason. Nothing will ever work between us if I don't trust you."

As he stared at her, his expression crestfallen, she went on in a rush, "Jason, I'm going to have a baby. I got pregnant Christmas Eve. That's why I've been pulling away. I was so scared that history would repeat itself—"

"Oh, good Lord!" Jason cried. "No wonder you reacted the way you did when you saw Tracy yesterday. My poor darling."

"I was just so afraid...afraid we wouldn't make it—"

"We're going to make it, darling," he said, clutching her tightly. His voice broke as he added, "And so is our child."

"I know," she agreed joyously. "I know we're going to make it now."

"Oh, Nickie, I'm so happy!"

They kissed, reveling in the glorious moment of reaffirmed love. Then Jason whispered against her hair, "You're sure you don't want me to close down the Galveston store?"

"Absolutely not," she said. "I don't want you to change the way you do anything."

"I'll take Tracy out of the fashion show," he said. "I promise."

"No, keep her in," Nickie said. Hugging him, she added quietly, "I trust you, Jason."

TWO HOURS LATER, they were back at Jason's condo. The minute the door closed behind them, they stared at each other lovingly, hungrily.

"It seems like forever," he said.

"I know," she replied.

He began unbuttoning her jacket. "I'm so thrilled about the baby."

A smile tugged at her lips. "Did you have any idea I was pregnant?"

He stroked her cheek tenderly. "Well, after Christmas, I certainly had my hopes. But I didn't want to crowd you about it, just when we were getting back together. I figured you'd tell me about it when you were ready."

"You know, you're really very dear," she said feelingly.

He pressed his lips to hers and continued unbuttoning her jacket. Then abruptly, he drew back, his expression anxious. "Did the doctor say making love is okay?"

She nodded. "You won't have to take cold showers for a while, anyway."

He laughed, drawing her close. "I'll be gentle with you, darling."

She ran her hand wickedly down the front of his trousers. "No promises here."

With a growl of pleasure, Jason swept her up into his arms, carrying her to the couch. "You're hell on a guy's honorable intentions."

She curled her arms around his neck and eyed him suggestively. "I just want us back together in every way."

"I know," he replied in a raspy whisper. He sat down on the couch with her in his lap, glancing askance at her heavy suit. "Now, how am I going to get you out of all this paraphernalia?"

She laughed. "I have every faith in your inventiveness."

THE OPENING of the newest branch of Stellar Attractions was a smashing success. The fashion show on Fat Tuesday was followed by free make-overs on Wednesday, draws for merchandise on Thursday and a lecture by a color expert on Friday. Traffic in the new store surpassed projections all week long.

On Saturday, free refreshments were served. Nickie and Jason stood near the front door, both dressed for a costume ball they'd be attending later. Jason looked irresistibly swashbuckling dressed as a pirate, his costume complete with a sexy black eye patch. Nickie appeared equally delightful in a Gauguin-inspired tropical gown.

The doorbell jangled constantly as tourists and islanders alike drifted in and out, exploring the shop and making numerous purchases. Jason's Mardi Gras collection—masks, beads and formal wear—was particularly popular with the crowd. Together, Jason and Nickie greeted the customers.

Often, Nickie glanced out the front windows, observing the rowdy merriment of Mardi Gras. The streets were packed with celebrants and vendors as the Hou Dah parade floated by. The parade participants, garishly attired as everything from fruits to insects to lampposts, tossed a constant spray of beads and doubloons into the chill February air, to the delight of the scrambling crowd.

"Happy, darling?" Jason asked, when there was at last a slow moment.

"Never happier," she replied.

"The dinner with your dad and Sandra last night was great," he remarked.

"Oh, I agree."

"You don't seem as resentful of your father as you used to be. Any reason for the change?"

She smiled. "I guess self-awareness—and love." Squeezing his hand, she added, "It sure doesn't leave much room in my heart for bitterness or mistrust—especially not when all I want there is you, and our baby."

"Oh, Nickie" Twirling his fake mustache, Jason said devilishly, "Keep talking like that, wench, and I'm going to drag you off to my ship."

Outside the window, a passing carnival clown wagged a finger and blew his noisemaker as he watched Galveston's newest, most dashing pirate grab his woman and kiss her.

Epilogue

JUST OVER A YEAR LATER, Jason and Nickie were again walking the Strand in Galveston, on a mild spring morning. This time, they were pushing a baby stroller with six-month-old Amanda Stellar strapped inside. Mandy had a shock of wavy brown hair, a heart-shaped mouth and big brown eyes. Today, she wore a pink T-shirt and tiny, matching jogging pants.

The threesome turned a corner and went past the Galveston store, watching a trio of shoppers go inside. "It's hard to believe the store has taken off so in just a year," Nickie remarked.

He winked at her. "It kind of kept pace with your stomach, huh, hon?"

Nickie screwed up her face at him. "You stinker." She looked down at the baby. "Mandy, why don't we attack him?"

Mandy Stellar waved her plump little arms and cooed up at her parents.

Jason grinned proudly. "You know, darling, she's you all over."

"Oh, brother," Nickie lamented. "Another little brown mouse turned loose in the world."

"Bite your tongue, woman," Jason growled. "I think you're both living dolls."

"Well, she's certainly a living doll, but I'm not so sure about me."

"*I'm* certain—always have been," Jason said solemnly.

"I guess you have," Nickie agreed with an adoring smile.

Jason leaned over toward the baby. "Right, Mandy? Isn't Mom the limit?"

Mandy was in the midst of gurgling again, when a siren blared out from around the corner; in mid-gurgle, she let out a frightened wail instead. At once, Jason unstrapped the baby, picked her up and held her against his shoulder. "It's all right, Mandy. Just a siren. Listen, it's gone now."

The tears were already drying on Mandy's face as she forgot her fright and turned her attention to playing with the buttons on her dad's shirt. Jason chuckled at the look of fierce concentration on the baby's face and smoothed down her soft curls. To Nickie, he remarked, "There's only one more thing I can think of that would make everything perfect."

"And what's that?" she demanded with mock indignation.

He grinned lecherously. "Well, we never did get to have the first baby of the New Year, like Richard and Meredith."

"What is this, Jason Stellar? One-upmanship in the maternity ward? What do you want to do now? Start having babies like new branches of your store?"

"Well, not exactly." Lowering his voice, he added, "But if we get busy right away, we might still make the front page, January first. You see, it's March now, and as I figure it, tonight's the deadline."

"And you told me *I* had a Machiavellian mind!" Nickie rolled her eyes and took the baby from Jason. "What do you think of this character, Mandy?"

The baby girl giggled her delight.

As Nickie placed Mandy back in the stroller, it occurred to her that she'd never in her life been happier. So many wonderful things had happened over the past year—like the night they'd both cried when they first held Mandy in the delivery room. True to his promises, Jason had kept his life in balance in every way; he was a wonderful father and husband. And she had lived up to her promise to trust him. Now, she couldn't wait to go home and try her best to provide Jason Stellar with the first baby of the *next* New Year.

Strapping Mandy in, Nickie smiled as she smoothed down the baby's little T-shirt, the one given her by her doting father that read, Newest Stellar Attraction.

HARLEQUIN Temptation

Rebels & Rogues

Jackson: Honesty was his policy...
and the price he demanded of the woman
he loved.

THE LAST HONEST MAN
by Leandra Logan
Temptation #393, May 1992

All men are not created equal. Some are
rough around the edges. Tough-minded but
tenderhearted. Incredibly sexy. The tempting
fulfillment of every woman's fantasy.

When it's time to fight for what they believe in,
to win that special woman, our Rebels and Rogues
are heroes at heart. Twelve Rebels and Rogues,
one each month in 1992, only from
Harlequin Temptation!

HARLEQUIN PROUDLY PRESENTS A
DAZZLING CONCEPT IN ROMANCE FICTION

One small town,
twelve terrific love stories.

TYLER—GREAT READING... GREAT SAVINGS... AND A FABULOUS FREE GIFT

Each book set in Tyler is a self-contained love story; together, the twelve novels stitch the fabric of the community.

By collecting proofs-of-purchase found in each Tyler book, you can receive a fabulous gift, ABSOLUTELY FREE! And use our special Tyler coupons to save on your next Tyler book purchase.

Join us for the third Tyler book, WISCONSIN WEDDING by Carla Neggers, available in May.

If you missed *Whirlwind* (March) or *Bright Hopes* (April) and would like to order them, send your name, address, zip or postal code, along with a check or money order for $3.99 (please do not send cash), plus 75¢ postage and handling ($1.00 in Canada) for each book ordered, payable to Harlequin Reader Service to:

In the U.S.	In Canada
3010 Walden Avenue	P.O. Box 609
P.O. Box 1325	Fort Erie, Ontario
Buffalo, NY 14269-1325	L2A 5X3

Please specify book title(s) with your order.

Canadian residents add applicable federal and provincial taxes.

TYLER-3

Following the success of WITH THIS RING,
Harlequin cordially invites you to enjoy the
romance of the wedding season with

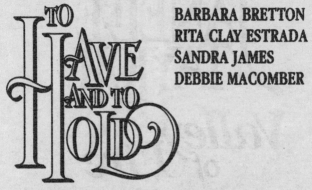

**BARBARA BRETTON
RITA CLAY ESTRADA
SANDRA JAMES
DEBBIE MACOMBER**

A collection of romantic stories that celebrate the joy,
excitement, and mishaps of planning that special day
by these four award-winning Harlequin authors.

**Available in April at your favorite Harlequin
retail outlets.**

® Harlequin®

JANELLE TAYLOR

Valley of Fire

HARLEQUIN IS PROUD TO PRESENT *VALLEY OF FIRE* BY JANELLE TAYLOR—AUTHOR OF TWENTY-TWO BOOKS, INCLUDING SIX *NEW YORK TIMES* BESTSELLERS

VALLEY OF FIRE—the warm and passionate story of Kathy Alexander, a famous romance author, and Steven Winngate, entrepreneur and owner of the magazine that intended to expose the real Kathy "Brandy" Alexander to her fans.

Don't miss VALLEY OF FIRE, available in May.

"GET AWAY FROM IT ALL" SWEEPSTAKES

HERE'S HOW THE SWEEPSTAKES WORKS

NO PURCHASE NECESSARY

To enter each drawing, complete the appropriate Official Entry Form or a 3" by 5" index card by hand-printing your name, address and phone number and the trip destination that the entry is being submitted for (i.e., Caneel Bay, Canyon Ranch or London and the English Countryside) and mailing it to: Get Away From It All Sweepstakes, P.O. Box 1397, Buffalo, New York 14269-1397.

No responsibility is assumed for lost, late or misdirected mail. Entries must be sent separately with first class postage affixed, and be received by: 4/15/92 for the Caneel Bay Vacation Drawing, 5/15/92 for the Canyon Ranch Vacation Drawing and 6/15/92 for the London and the English Countryside Vacation Drawing. Sweepstakes is open to residents of the U.S. (except Puerto Rico) and Canada, 21 years of age or older as of 5/31/92.

For complete rules send a self-addressed, stamped (WA residents need not affix return postage) envelope to: Get Away From It All Sweepstakes, P.O. Box 4892, Blair, NE 68009.

© 1992 HARLEQUIN ENTERPRISES LTD.   SWP-RLS

"GET AWAY FROM IT ALL" SWEEPSTAKES

HERE'S HOW THE SWEEPSTAKES WORKS

NO PURCHASE NECESSARY

To enter each drawing, complete the appropriate Official Entry Form or a 3" by 5" index card by hand-printing your name, address and phone number and the trip destination that the entry is being submitted for (i.e., Caneel Bay, Canyon Ranch or London and the English Countryside) and mailing it to: Get Away From It All Sweepstakes, P.O. Box 1397, Buffalo, New York 14269-1397.

No responsibility is assumed for lost, late or misdirected mail. Entries must be sent separately with first class postage affixed, and be received by: 4/15/92 for the Caneel Bay Vacation Drawing, 5/15/92 for the Canyon Ranch Vacation Drawing and 6/15/92 for the London and the English Countryside Vacation Drawing. Sweepstakes is open to residents of the U.S. (except Puerto Rico) and Canada, 21 years of age or older as of 5/31/92.

For complete rules send a self-addressed, stamped (WA residents need not affix return postage) envelope to: Get Away From It All Sweepstakes, P.O. Box 4892, Blair, NE 68009.

© 1992 HARLEQUIN ENTERPRISES LTD.   SWP-RLS

"GET AWAY FROM IT ALL"

Brand-new Subscribers-Only Sweepstakes

OFFICIAL ENTRY FORM

This entry must be received by: May 15, 1992
This month's winner will be notified by: May 31, 1992
Trip must be taken between: June 30, 1992—June 30, 1993

YES, I want to win the Canyon Ranch vacation for two. I understand the prize includes round-trip airfare and the two additional prizes revealed in the BONUS PRIZES insert.

Name _____

Address _____

City _____

State/Prov. _____ Zip/Postal Code_____

Daytime phone number _____
(Area Code)

Return entries with invoice in envelope provided. Each book in this shipment has two entry coupons — and the more coupons you enter, the better your chances of winning!
© 1992 HARLEQUIN ENTERPRISES LTD.   2M-CPN

"GET AWAY FROM IT ALL"

Brand-new Subscribers-Only Sweepstakes

OFFICIAL ENTRY FORM

This entry must be received by: May 15, 1992
This month's winner will be notified by: May 31, 1992
Trip must be taken between: June 30, 1992—June 30, 1993

YES, I want to win the Canyon Ranch vacation for two. I understand the prize includes round-trip airfare and the two additional prizes revealed in the BONUS PRIZES insert.

Name _____

Address _____

City _____

State/Prov. _____ Zip/Postal Code_____

Daytime phone number _____
(Area Code)

Return entries with invoice in envelope provided. Each book in this shipment has two entry coupons — and the more coupons you enter, the better your chances of winning!
© 1992 HARLEQUIN ENTERPRISES LTD.   2M-CPN